LOVING STRANGER

LOVING STRANGER

Louise Pakeman

CHIVERS
THORNDIKE

This Large Print edition is published by BBC Audiobooks Ltd, Bath, England and by Thorndike Press®, Waterville, Maine, USA.

Published in 2004 in the U.K. by arrangement with Dorian Literary Agency.

Published in 2004 in the U.S. by arrangement with Dorian Literary Agency.

U.K. Hardcover ISBN 0–7540–9980–6 (Chivers Large Print)
U.K. Softcover ISBN 0–7540–9981–4 (Camden Large Print)
U.S. Softcover ISBN 0–7862–6376–8 (Nightingale)

The text of this Large Print edition is unabridged.
Other aspects of the book may vary from the original edition.

Set in 16 pt. New Times Roman.

Printed in Great Britain on acid-free paper.

British Library Cataloguing in Publication Data available

Library of Congress Cataloging-in-Publication Data

Pakeman, Louise, 1936–
    Loving stranger / by Louise Pakeman.
       p.   cm.
    ISBN 0–7862–6376–8 (lg. print : sc : alk. paper)
    1. Strangers—Fiction. 2. Large type books. I. Title.
PR9619.4.P35L68 2004
823'.92—dc22   2003071129

CHAPTER ONE

'You know that advertisement I answered a couple of weeks ago?' Linda Weston reminded, rather than asked, her friend and room-mate, Sandra, as she picked up an envelope almost hidden by the groceries on the kitchen table.

The girls had collected the mail from their box as they came back from the supermarket with their usual Friday night supplies.

'Well, it looks as if there is a reply here.'

Flopping down in one of the shabby, but comfy, armchairs in the kitchen-cum-living-room of their apartment, she began to tear open the envelope, ignoring the knife that the more tidy Sandra was offering.

'What did I tell you?' Linda exclaimed triumphantly. 'There's loads of jobs—look.'

She brandished the letter in Sandra's direction.

'We can take our pick! Boy, what a way to see the world, all at someone else's expense, actually being paid to travel! Think of it. We—'

She tailed off as it dawned on her she was not getting the enthusiastic response she had expected from Sandy.

'You haven't changed your mind have you?' she asked.

Sandra shook her head slowly.

1

'No, I haven't changed my mind because I never made it up. I didn't say I wanted to go to Australia. You were the one who got all enthused about the idea when you read that advertisement from that agency. I'm not enthused, not at all. I don't particularly want to go to Australia.'

'Why not? I thought you were as keen as I was. I thought you thought it was a good idea?'

'Yes! You thought! I never said,' Sandra pointed out. 'As it happens, I'm not that keen on the idea, and I don't think I would like Australia.'

'Why ever not? It's a wonderful country—young, vital, a place where the sun shines! Not like here.'

Linda swept a hand in the general direction of the window in a disparaging sweep that both took in, and dismissed the gathering gloom of an early autumn evening.

'Maybe a more accurate description would be a brash country without much culture, and damned hot! Anyway, it doesn't matter what it's like, it has one huge disadvantage as far as I am concerned. It's on the wrong side of the world!'

Sandra smiled at her friend.

'Forget it, Lin. You'll get another job. You don't have to chase off to the ends of the earth!'

Linda smiled wryly, appreciating the tact that had made Sandra say, 'You'll get another

2

job,' rather than 'another boyfriend.'

'Sandy, I don't want you to think I don't appreciate what you've done for me these last few months, or that I'm taking off and leaving you. I just feel that I need to get right away— start afresh—and this seems such a good opportunity, but I still wish you were coming with me. Won't you please think about it?'

Sandra shook her head slowly.

'No,' she said, 'I'm sorry, Linda, but I just feel it's not the thing for me and I am not at all sure it is for you either. Or perhaps it's that you are not going in the right spirit.'

'What do you mean?'

Linda jerked the words out defensively, raising her head and unconsciously jutting her chin.

'Well,' her friend answered slowly and hesitantly, 'it seems to me as if you are getting away from England rather than going to Australia.'

She smiled wryly. 'In another time and place you might have gone into a convent! But Australia isn't a convent, you know!'

'You mean,' Linda retorted, 'that I'll find there are those awful things, men, there, too! Don't worry, Sandy, they won't bother me because I just don't care about them any more!'

*   *   *

3

Struggling through Customs, immigration and the awesome business of arriving in a strange country alone, Linda remembered Sandy's words breaking through jet-lag haze urging her to forget it. For the first time she wished with all her heart she had taken her friend's advice and stayed put!

When the moment came for her to go through that last door and face the crowd of friends and relations waiting for the passengers she would, had it been at all possible, have simply turned tail and got back on the plane. Too late she remembered that she had forgotten to label herself and only hoped the person meeting her had not done likewise.

Then she saw him, just when she was on the point of pushing the panic button. A tall man in blue denims and a check shirt was eyeing her speculatively. Fastened to the shirt was a label saying BLUEGUMS. She had been instructed to wear a label with her name on but was told that the person meeting her would wear the name of the property, as it might be any one of several people detailed to pick her up at the airport. Assuming a confidence she was far from feeling, she made her way through the crowds to the stranger.

'I'm Linda.'

His gaze travelled slowly from her face to her feet and halfway back up before he replied.

'I guessed you might be, even though you are not labelled.'

He took off his own label as he spoke. There was something slightly admonishing in his tone and Linda found herself mumbling an apology. Ignoring, or just not noticing, her outstretched hand he reached for her largest case.

'This the lot?'

She nodded in reply.

'We'd best get going then.'

Grabbing up the remainder of her bags as best she could, Linda found herself meekly trotting after him out of the terminal building and towards the carpark.

As she stepped out of the air-conditioned building she would have stopped in her tracks were she not afraid of losing sight of her companion who was striding on ahead. Never before had the air outside felt so tangible. It was as if she was walking into a warm blanket.

She gave a sigh of relief as she climbed up into the passenger seat of the four-wheel drive vehicle that he eventually led her to almost on the far side of the vast carpark. Pushing back her hair she could feel the beads of perspiration on her forehead.

The man in the driver's seat turned and grinned at her as he fitted the key in the ignition.

'Hot?' he asked.

Linda nodded.

'We haven't got into the summer proper yet,' he informed her with more satisfaction than sympathy. 'Give it another couple of months then it will be hot.'

'There was a frost the night before I left home and it looked as if snow was on the way.'

Linda felt a sudden need to explain her whimpish reaction to the heat. As they left the carpark, Linda settled down to her first taste of Australia. She looked inquiringly at her companion as he swung the vehicle not towards the city of Melbourne but out towards the open country.

As if in reply to her unspoken query he said, 'We're heading north, to Bluegums,' he told her.

'Oh,' was about the most intelligent reply Linda was able to summon.

Expecting to go into the city as that was where all the correspondence had come from she was finding it curiously difficult to adjust her thinking in the dream-like state that the long flight had brought on. Once again the what-am-I-doing-here feeling swept through her. She did not even know her companion's name!

When, for the second time, he answered her question before she asked it, Linda thought wildly that she must be thinking out loud, even though she couldn't remember hearing her own voice!

'I guess you would like to know who you are

6

travelling with?' he asked without taking his eyes off the road ahead, or waiting for her reply. 'My name is Rod, short for Roderick, but everyone calls me Bluey,' he told her.

'Oh.'

Once again Linda found the monosyllable was all she could muster, though she did wonder why anyone with such a perfectly good name should be given the nickname Bluey.

'On account of my hair,' he explained, which only left her more confused.

Half turning towards her he flashed her a grin.

'It's an old Aussie custom,' he told her. 'People with reddish hair usually get dubbed Bluey. If it bothers you, call me Rod.'

She managed a smile. There was so much she wanted to ask him but her mind seemed to have turned to cotton wool. She would enjoy the unfamiliar scenery for a while. Soon, she found herself dozing off.

She came to with a slight shiver. It was certainly not cold, just cooler. The sun had gone and dusk was enveloping them as they turned in through a gateway with what appeared to be an ancient fridge standing by the gatepost. A kilometre or so later, Rod pulled up in front of a large, single storey weatherboard house.

The biggest dog Linda had ever seen lay stretched on the veranda. She later learned he was a cross between a Great Dane and a

Mastiff. As if aware that he had been caught napping, literally of doing his guard duty, he raised his head and barked without bothering to get to his feet.

Feeling reluctant to face the enormous creature, Linda stayed firmly put. To her chagrin Rod had seen and was amused.

'Don't worry about Tarquin,' he told her. 'His bark is definitely worse than his bite!'

At the sound of his voice, the huge animal lumbered to his feet and hurtled down the veranda steps towards them.

'This,' Rod said, 'is Linda!'

She looked round thinking someone else must have materialised out of the shadows, then realised he was talking to the dog.

'Just so that he knows you next time he sees you and doesn't try to eat you!' he explained as he turned back to the vehicle to help her with her bags.

Too tired to retaliate, she pulled out the rest of her luggage and followed him up the steps to the house, the big dog padding at her side. As Rod pushed open the door, Tarquin flopped back down on the veranda boards to resume his interrupted slumber.

Linda found herself in a wide, central hall with doors it seemed, radiating off it in all directions. From behind one of these came the sound of voices. After a few seconds, she realised it was a TV playing.

'I'll show you your room then introduce you

8

to Ronnie,' he told her leading the way to a door halfway down the hall.

He opened the door and switched on the light to reveal a comfortably, but plainly furnished bedroom. He dumped her case on the floor and indicated that she should do likewise with the bags that she carried and then follow him.

Behind the closed door of the room where the TV played, Linda found, not another man as she had expected from the name, but a cosy, grey-haired, grandmotherly woman, snoring gently in front of the blaring set. She sat up with a start when they entered the room.

'You are back in good time,' she said, adding, 'I didn't expect you yet!'

Linda was just thinking that she looked about as guilty at being caught dozing as Tarquin when Rod, in that uncanny way he seemed to have of reading her thoughts, or at least thinking the same thing at the same time, said, 'You and Tarquin are a great pair to leave in charge! He was asleep, too, when we arrived!'

His smile softened his remark, which was obviously taken in good part. He turned to Linda.

'This is Veronica Baker, otherwise known as Ronnie, which is another reason why they called me Bluey. Too confusing to have a Ron and a Rod in one house!'

The older woman scrambled to her feet,

9

smiling and holding out her hand to Linda.

'I expect you are feeling hungry and tired. Come along into the kitchen and have something then you can have a shower and get a good night's rest before seeing what you have let yourself in for!'

Linda was tired, too tired to feel anything more than a mild curiosity at these words. Fed and showered, however, she lay wakeful listening to the strange night sounds. She might be on another planet, not just on the other side of the world, and she found herself wondering what, indeed, she had let herself in for!

However, her restless mind could not control her young, healthy body and it seemed as if she had barely closed her eyes before they were opening to bright sunshine breaking through the curtains. She lay for a while gathering her wandering thoughts and recollecting the events of the last twenty-four hours.

With a mixture of curiosity and nervous apprehension tingling her nerve ends she dressed quickly and made her way to the kitchen which seemed to be the hub of the household. She found Rod, or Bluey as she was already beginning to think of him, just about to start on what appeared to be a breakfast for a giant which Ronnie was just setting in front of him.

Though they both turned to her with a

smile, somehow Linda was sure that she had interrupted a discussion about herself.

'Er—good morning!' she said and endeavoured to sound confident.

'Hello, my dear!' Ronnie replied, sounding warm and welcoming. 'Come and have some breakfast. I hope you had a good night.'

'Hi!' was Bluey's laconic greeting, fork raised in salute.

'Sit down, make yourself at home. Now what would you like for breakfast? The same as Blue?' Ronnie asked.

Linda glanced across at the loaded plate and managed to suppress a shudder.

'Oh, no—no thanks! Just coffee and toast will do!'

'Have some cereal.'

Ronnie pushed a packet across the table.

'Keep up your strength!'

Bluey's grin was disarming and Linda quipped back, 'What for?' Then suddenly serious she added, 'To be truthful, I don't really have much idea what I am supposed to do or why I am here.'

She tailed off rather weakly looking with unconscious appeal at her two companions and dropping into a chair at the table. She pulled the cereal packet closer and rather absently helped herself.

'What did you think you were coming to do?' Bluey asked.

'Well, the advertisement was for someone to

11

run an office and the address was in Melbourne.'

'So, you came all the way to Australia to work in a nice, tidy city office and you find yourself way up in the outback with nary an office in sight! Didn't you find out any more before you took flight?'

Bluey's tone stung her into a quick retort.

'I had no reason to doubt that I was expected to work in a city office. Though I was told when I applied that I must be prepared to do anything and there would be some travel involved I didn't expect to travel the minute I got off the plane.'

She looked directly across the table at Bluey, her sudden anger and irritation making her hazel eyes flash in what was, had she known it, a most attractive way.

'Perhaps you can enlighten me, as you brought me here, apparently under orders.'

Bluey chewed on the last mouthful of his breakfast, pushed his plate across the table and leaned back in his chair before he answered.

'Well, now, it will probably surprise you to know that there is an office here for you, all equipped with computer and everything. You can do pretty well what you like in it just so long as you keep all the farm records and accounts straight. As for the other things you will have to do, well, that depends. As the jillaroo round here, it will be anything I, or

12

Ronnie, wants help with!'

The grin he flashed her as he pushed his coffee mug over for a refill was anything but calming. Linda, feeling her dander rise, asked, 'And what, pray, is a jillaroo?'

Seeing that he was getting to her, Bluey looked serious, except for those dazzling blue eyes that held an irrepressible sparkle.

'A female jackaroo, of course,' he offered laconically by way of explanation, feeling pretty sure that she would not know what that was either.

He was wrong. She may not have a very precise idea of the duties of a jackaroo but she had read something about them somewhere and the memory was slowly surfacing.

'Aha, yes, a jillaroo will be what we would call a girl Friday.'

Linda took a long sip of her coffee then looked across the table at this person who, she suddenly realised, in spite of his power to needle her, had a vitality about him that she was forced to admit had a certain attraction.

'And which of many duties am I expected to perform today?'

He answered her with a question, of sorts. The way he said it, Linda thought, made it sound more like a rather negative statement than a question.

'Can you ride a horse?' was his enquiry.

'Yes,' she answered shortly.

She was gratified by the brief flash of

13

surprise on his face but mortified by his mumbled, 'Oh, well, we'll see. You can come with me. I've got some stock work to do. Change your clothes and I'll see you outside in half an hour!'

Linda rummaged through her clothes till she found the jodhpurs that, truth to tell, she had only thrown in at the last moment because what she wasn't packing was going to the nearest charity shop and they had cost her so much that she couldn't just chuck them out like that. She pulled them on and hunted for a shirt that didn't look too crumpled after the long trip. Then she found the most sensible pair of shoes she could and went out to meet Bluey.

He looked at her in undisguised amusement when she appeared. His eyes ran up and down her trim figure taking in all the curves as well as the clothes. Linda felt very exposed.

'No hat?' was all he said.

'It was too bulky. I couldn't get it in the case,' she told him, thinking of the smart black riding hat she had left behind.

'No boots?' he asked then.

Once more she shook her head, and replied, 'I usually wore these plain walking shoes to ride in,' she told him defensively, feeling more and more that she wasn't coming up to scratch in his eyes.

'You'll have to get some boots,' he told her, 'and a hat. Ronnie can lend you one

14

today probably.'

He strode to the door and called out.

'Ronnie, are you there? Can you lend our new jillaroo a hat or she'll come back like a pickled prawn.'

Linda felt an angry flush creeping up her neck and staining her cheeks so that she did, probably, look like a pickled prawn already. The man, she decided, was a typically crude Aussie with no manners at all!

Ronnie appeared in the doorway holding a battered felt hat with a broad brim and a cord to go under the chin. She handed it to Bluey calling out to Linda as she did so, 'This should keep the sun off you for today.'

Then, just as he had, she let her eyes travel down Linda's body resting on the neat, tightly-fitting jodhpurs.

'You're going to be hot enough as it is,' she warned.

Linda clamped the hat down on her head and immediately felt grateful for its shade. At least she could see where she was going now! She wondered fleetingly if she would ever get used to the ferocity of this sun. Her thoughts were cut short by Bluey's voice.

'Coming?'

She followed him out to the back to what she would have called a small paddock but he called a yard. A group of horses was idling under the shade of what she learned later was a peppercorn tree. Bluey eyed her

15

speculatively then handed her one of the headstalls he had in his hand.

'You'd better have old Molly. She's the little skewbald. She'll look after you.'

He nodded in the direction of the horses who were now eyeing them, no doubt wondering which of them was required to work today. Linda accepted the headstall and followed Bluey through the gate.

Somehow she hadn't expected things to be quite so hands-on from the word go. To date, her riding had been done at a riding school where the horse was presented to you all ready to go.

'The gate!' Bluey yelled at her. 'Shut the gate or they'll all be out!'

Annoyed at herself, she turned back to the gate which, preoccupied with her own thoughts, she hadn't thought to shut. Hastily she slammed it shut and then found she couldn't work the fastening, a crude, wire loop that slid over the gate-post—or would slide over if it were larger or she were stronger.

She heard a grunt of exasperation somewhere near her ear then a strong brown arm reached over, a hand took hold of the loop and slipped it over the post. This was only the first of the many incidents that revealed her ineptitude. Molly was the cause of the next humiliation. She wouldn't let her catch her. Once again Bluey had to come to her rescue.

'Don't wave the headstall in her face like

16

that. Be a bit more subtle. Get to the side of her and put it under her chin and slide it over her nose—so,' he told her, doing just that while the wretched horse stood like an angel.

He handed the end of the rope to Linda.

'Now, tie her up to the fence.'

Linda was about to do that when she realised that he meant on the other side, outside the yard. She followed Bluey meekly through the gate wishing herself a million miles away—back in England at a comfortable office desk to be precise!

She followed Bluey into a dim, dusty tack-room smelling of horse, leather and hay and looked round in amazement at the assortment of saddles on the racks—heavy, clumsy-looking saddles like nothing she had ever seen before. She staggered slightly beneath the weight when he handed one to her then casually threw a bridle across it.

'OK, there's your stuff. Oh, hang on. You need a saddle blanket!'

A dusty blanket square came winging her way to land on the stuff already over her arm. Not quite sure what to do with this load of gear, she went on standing there, waiting for Bluey to collect his own gear. She then followed him back out into the sun.

Somehow she managed to get it on to Molly's back and then by carefully watching what Bluey did and being just one stage behind, she had her saddled up, but not bridled. It was only when she was looking speculatively at the mare's head and then at the gear that had to go on it that she saw her eye, or rather saw that one eye didn't appear to be there!

'Bluey!'

Her voice sounded high-pitched with anxiety.

'Something is wrong with Molly's eye!'

'No,' he told her. 'She's one-eyed, that's all!'

'All!' Linda's voice was a definite squeak now. 'Is she safe? How did it happen?'

'Barley grass probably. They get the spikes in their eyes and if no-one notices it in time, then they lose the eye.'

He sounded as if it was the most natural thing in the world to have a horse with one eye.

'But don't you worry about her. Old Molly sees more with one eye than most horses do with two. Better get her bridled up. Leave the headstall on, in case we need to tie them up.'

Linda left the headstall on but unclipped the lead rope. Instantly Molly stepped away from the rails and would have gone if Blue hadn't moved quickly and grabbed her headstall. Quickly he retied her.

'Now put the bridle on,' he told Linda.

When she didn't move, he took it from her with the same grunt of irritation he had made before and, holding the bit beneath Molly's mouth, deftly prised it open and slipped the bit between her teeth and the headpiece over her ears. Linda wondered if she would ever be able to do that. He undid the rope and knotted it round the animal's neck then turned to the saddle and checked the girth.

He turned to look over his shoulder and grinned at her as he tightened it at least four holes.

'Good job I looked at that for you!' he told her. 'OK. Get on!'

Linda looked at the saddle. It was quite unlike any saddle she had ever seen before, heavy and deep-seated with bits sticking up and out of it. On the breath of a sigh she moved forward and while Bluey held the mare's head managed to hoist herself aloft. He looked at her critically, or it seemed so to Linda.

'Your stirrup leathers are too short,' he told her.

'They seem about the same length I usually have them,' she protested, keeping her feet firmly in the strange, heavy-looking stirrups.

He tried to move her leg so that he could alter the buckle on the leather but she moved her foot slightly to stop him and involuntarily touched the old mare into action. Bluey shrugged.

'Suit yourself! But I reckon you'll want them lengthening before long!' Turning away to his own horse, he swung up lightly into the saddle.

'You can ride the old girl on a looser rein

than that!' he suggested over his shoulder as she followed him out of the yard. 'Just sit there. She knows what to do!'

Linda, too busy trying to adjust herself to the strange saddle and the gait of the horse beneath her merely nodded. Truth to tell she was not at all sure she could do anything anyway!

CHAPTER TWO

As she jogged up beside Bluey's gaunt grey, he looked down at her and commented, 'Old Molly isn't a follower. Always likes to be up front.'

With each step, Linda was feeling less in charge. She couldn't remember any of the riding school horses back in England having such dominant personalities. It wasn't long before her knees were beginning to feel stiff and what she thought of as the front bumps on the saddle were digging into her.

'I've never seen a saddle with bits sticking up like these,' she remarked after a while. 'What are they for?'

'If you don't know now, you will by the time we get back!' he told her, grinning at her. 'They're to help keep you in the saddle. Something they would do a good deal better if you had let me adjust your leathers.'

'Oh!' Linda replied while her mind quickly made up to ask Bluey if he could adjust her leathers.

Bluey merely reined in his horse and instructed her how to lengthen her stirrup leathers by at least two holes without dismounting. Feeling totally at Molly's mercy, she followed his instructions and was relieved to find that with the longer stirrups, her thighs fitted comfortably between the padded bumps and she did indeed feel a lot more secure in the saddle.

'Better?' he asked as they moved forward again.

'Much!' she assured him with feeling. 'I've never seen a saddle like this before.'

'It's an Australian stock saddle, designed to keep you in place in relative comfort all day. Once you get used to it you will never want to ride on anything else.'

He reined in as he spoke and pointed to a mob of cattle in the distance.

'See those steers over there? We have to move them into the next paddock. Quite a simple job. I'll ride round this side of them and open the gate then I'll come back and bring them along from this side. You take the other side and send them up from there. If you don't know what to do, leave it to Molly. You shouldn't have any trouble but if she has to turn fast you'll be glad of those pads!'

Bluey kicked his horse into a canter and made a wide sweep round the cattle towards the gate on the far side. For a brief moment, Linda found herself watching in sheer pleasure as man and horse, looking almost like one being, moved swiftly away from her then the need to exert some sort of control over her own mount took all her attention.

By the time the whole herd was through the gate, Linda, dishevelled and breathless, was hanging on to the saddle and was very definitely a passenger, not a rider.

'I guess you know what those bumps on the saddle are for now?'

Bluey looked up at her from the ground as he turned back to his horse after fastening the gate they had just driven the cattle through.

Too breathless to speak, she nodded in reply. He swung himself back into the saddle as she added, 'And I also know what you mean about Molly knowing what to do. I feel I was somewhat superfluous to the whole operation!'

They rode back in a silence that was more friendly. Linda was still too exhausted to make light conversation and any other sort seemed unnecessary. Bluey, she had to admit, was kind enough not to comment on her riding ability, or the lack of it.

When they finally dismounted in the yard, her legs felt at the same time both stiff and wobbly and she could hardly muster the strength to hoist the heavy saddle off the mare's back. Under Bluey's guidance she removed the gear, gave Molly a quick rub down and turned her out in the yard.

'I guess it must be getting on for lunch time,' Bluey commented as she followed in his wake towards the house.

She stopped involuntarily when she saw a flashy car drawn up outside the house. The expensive model looked strangely out of place.

Not even the coating of dust could make it look at home. Bluey tuned to her and raised an eyebrow.

'Looks as if our boss is here,' he told her.

Though there was nothing in his voice that betrayed his true feeling, Linda was left with the impression that he wasn't particularly pleased to see the car. Certainly she herself would much rather have met her new employer when she was a little more presentable.

She would have dearly loved to escape to her bedroom when they got to the house, or at the very least to the bathroom, but as they entered the cool dimness of the hallway she came face to face with a strikingly good-looking man in his late thirties, dressed impeccably for the country in the way a city person would dress.

Linda was acutely conscious of the grease from Molly's coat on her hands, the tight jodhpurs that felt as if they were glued to her legs and the dust that seemed to cover her from head to foot. She pulled off the wide-brimmed hat and put up her hand to push her hair back, leaving a trail of sweat and grime across her face. Mercifully for her composure, she was unaware of this.

'Hi, Bluey! Everything OK?'

Without waiting for an answer he turned to Linda.

'You must be Linda.'

He held out a hand and turned on her a smile of such dazzling charm that she felt her knees, already wobbly, turn to water. She took the proffered hand and mumbled that, yes, she was indeed Linda.

'All the way from England!' her new boss remarked, still smiling. 'I'm Derek Ford,' he added, finally releasing her hand.

'How do you do, Mr Ford?' Linda responded primly, and even as she spoke, she caught the glint of amusement in Bluey's eyes.

'Please, it's Derek. You're in Australia now, the classless land,' he replied.

She stood there tongue-tied, her hand still in his wondering how to escape and get out of the uncomfortable clothes and tidy herself. Even as she thought this, her hand was dropped abruptly and Derek Ford turned away from her to talk to Bluey about the farm.

Thankfully Linda headed for the door. As she shot down the hall she heard a child's voice coming from the kitchen. Then just as she reached the bathroom door, it opened and what she could only describe as an astonishing vision came out.

If Linda had been aware of her appearance when she confronted Derek Ford, she was even more so on meeting Marcia. Tall, willowy, perfectly dressed in designer jeans and tailored shirt, perfectly coiffed and immaculately manicured and made-up, she was accompanied by a wave of perfume that was definitely not cheap.

'Why, hello! You must be the new girl Derek just brought out from England.'

The words were cordial enough but the tone was condescending.

Feeling at a distinct disadvantage Linda merely nodded and mumbled, 'Yes,' before beating a hasty retreat into the bathroom.

When she saw her flushed and dust-smudged face and dishevelled hair, her self confidence dropped. She turned the taps on full blast and cleaned herself with angry vigour. Back in her room she peeled off the jodhpurs and chucked them in a corner before pulling on a pair of jeans, good, but definitely not designer, and a clean shirt.

After running a comb through her hair, dusting her face lightly with powder and touching her lips with a soft rose lipstick she felt more confident. Unsure quite what to do she supposed she had better present herself. She paused in the hall. From the lounge came the sound of male voices punctuated now and then by that of a woman and from the kitchen she could hear a child prattling and Ronnie answering. She opted for the kitchen.

Ronnie was putting the finishing touches to a cold lunch laid out on the table in the dining area. A child, perched on a high stool at the breakfast bar, was already eating. She waved a spoon cheerily at Linda.

'Hi, I'm Jessica. Are you Daddy's new girl

26

from England?'

'Hello, yes, I am.' Then turning to Ronnie she asked, 'Is there anything I can do to help?'

'Tell the others that lunch is ready, if you will,' the housekeeper replied.

As she crossed the hall on her mission, Linda's confidence was somewhat buoyed by Jessica announcing in her clear young voice, 'She looks nice!'

Ronnie had prepared a simple but very satisfying meal of cold meats, salads and cheeses, washed down with cool beer and followed by coffee. Linda found that she was hungry after the morning's work and did full justice to the food. She wished, however, that she had opted for orange juice instead of beer as she felt her senses dull and her lids grow heavy.

It would have been easier to stay alert if she had been able to take part in the conversation round the lunch table but Derek and Marcia were talking to Bluey about things, and people, she knew nothing about and Ronnie seemed fully occupied seeing that everyone at the table and the child on the stool had all they needed.

Suddenly she realised that there was a lull in the conversation and everyone seemed to be looking at her.

'Sorry?' she mumbled, more as an enquiry than anything else, and looked at the faces round the table.

Bluey grinned at her in evident amusement.

'I think Linda is still suffering from jet-lag,' he remarked.

'Could be you worked her too hard, too soon!' Ronnie put in.

Linda could not summon a reply to either of them and sat there in silence. What, she wondered, had happened to her wits since she got to this country. She, who had always prided herself on her ready and quick repartee, seemed unable to summon up an answer to anything! It was, to her surprise, Marcia who came to her rescue.

'If you dragged her out round the stock this morning and she only arrived yesterday, I'm not a bit surprised she's bushed, Bluey. You're a slave-driver! I hope you aren't planning more work for her this afternoon. She looks to me as if she needs a rest.'

While Linda did not particularly like being discussed as if she were an inanimate object, the prospect of resting was tempting indeed. She looked across the table gratefully at Marcia hoping to catch her eye and show her gratitude with a smile, but she was looking at Bluey waiting for his response. Linda looked to her boss. Before she could frame a question or request he nodded.

'Good idea! Take a couple of hours to catch up,' he said to her.

Feeling rather like a child who has been excused, or dismissed, from the table Linda pushed back her chair and headed for her room. Looking at her belongings still half unpacked, she fully intended to tidy up but sheer drowsiness made her flop down on the bed. After pulling down the blind to keep out the fierce afternoon sun and switching on the small fan that stood on the chest near the bed, she began to doze. The last sound she heard was a woman's tinkling laugh.

When she opened her eyes and looked at her watch, Linda was amazed to see that she had slept for over two hours. For a few minutes she couldn't think where she was but as realisation flooded back she slid off the bed and padded across the room to the door.

She opened it a chink and listened. There was no sound, only the unmistakable stillness of an empty house. Turning back into the room she set about the task of hanging her clothes up in the closet and generally making the place her own.

She had just closed the last drawer when she heard a vehicle drive up, a car door slam and voices outside. Moving to the window, she saw Bluey get out of the driving seat of the four-wheel drive and first Derek then Marcia climb down on the passenger side followed by Jessica who had apparently been riding in the back.

She was about to turn back into the room when she heard another vehicle arrive. It was Ronnie driving a station wagon. She parked as near the door as she could get then began to unload cardboard boxes and plastic supermarket bags, obviously filled with groceries. Linda felt a momentary regret that she had been asleep and not gone with her.

She supposed, as everybody seemed to be back at the house, she had better put in an appearance. Hastily she tidied her hair, slipped her feet into comfortable flat shoes and headed for the kitchen. Ronnie was just dumping an armful of shopping on the bench when she walked in.

'Hi. Had a good rest?'

'Very, thanks! But I feel a bit guilty sleeping while you have been doing all this shopping!'

'I'll take you along with me next time, don't worry. In the meantime maybe you could bring the last load in from the back of the station wagon, please?'

Linda was only too glad to have something definite to do, however small a task and hurried out to bring in the last of the bags and boxes.

'Phew!' she exclaimed as she dropped them down on the breakfast bar. 'You look as if you have stocked up for a siege!'

'Something like that!' The older woman smiled at her. 'Fact is I never know how many I have to cater for or for how long when Derek turns up!'

'Can I help you with anything?'

'Well, you can't put the stuff away as you don't know where it all goes, but you can put the electric kettle on as I expect everybody will want a cup of tea. That includes myself. How about you?'

'That sounds the best offer I have had for ages!' she said as she took the jug to the sink to fill it up.

Ronnie nodded towards a glass-fronted cupboard running along one wall.

'Use the big tea-pot,' she instructed. 'The caddy is over there and you will find a cake tin with some cookies in the pantry cupboard.'

By the time Ronnie had finished putting away her supplies, Linda had tea made and put out cups and saucers together with a plate of home-made cookies. She was just about to ask where to take it when everyone tramped into the kitchen.

'Good, tea!' Derek exclaimed, rubbing his hands.

Marcia took a small tray down and pointedly laid it with three cups and saucers, milk and sugar, poured the tea and took it through to the lounge, followed by Derek. Bluey shrugged, grinned at Ronnie and helped himself to one of the cookies.

'I don't need to watch my figure!' he said as he followed the other two, almost colliding with the child as she bounded into the kitchen.

Jessica clambered up on to one of the stools and dived straight into the cookies.

'Ooh—good! Choc chip! I love these, Ronnie!'

Linda pulled up another stool opposite Jessica and smiled across at her.

'How old are you, Jessica?' she asked.

'Six. Look, I've lost a tooth!'

She opened a crumbly mouth to reveal a large gap in her top teeth.

'Did the tooth fairy come?' Ronnie enquired.

'Of course. She left me two dollars!'

'Two dollars! My word, the rate for teeth has gone up a lot lately.'

Linda leaned her elbows on the table and sipped her tea, gratefully pondering the relationships in this household she had come across the world to join. Impossible to question Ronnie with the child sitting opposite her.

She occupied herself that evening by helping Ronnie prepare the evening meal and supervising Jessica getting to bed and reading her a story once she was there. Marcia, she thought, seemed very unconcerned about the child. Even so it didn't occur to her that she was not her mother until she was tucking Jessica in and saying good-night to her.

'I like you, Linda,' the little girl said suddenly. 'I wish you lived with us in Melbourne instead of Marcia!'

Back in the kitchen, with Ronnie, Linda asked, 'Is Marcia Jessica's mother?'

'Jessica's mother! Good heavens, no! She is just the latest in a succession of—well, I don't know quite how to describe them!'

'Poor child!' Linda said sympathetically. 'It must be a bit rough for her. Seems a nice kid, too!'

'Oh, she is. I've got a lot of time for Jessica. I don't really know how she manages to be such a balanced sort of child with her most unstable background!'

Ronnie suddenly tailed off into silence and following her glance, Linda saw Derek Ford standing in the doorway. She wondered how long he had been there.

'Could I have a word with you, Linda, in the office?' he said quietly.

Linda followed him to the room built on to the back of the house which was the farm office. Derek waved his hand in an all-embracing gesture around the room and as she followed its sweep, she saw a pile of envelopes on the table. Most of them looked like bills.

'Tomorrow I would like you to get things straight here. Answer anything urgent, get bills paid and such, before we leave for Melbourne.'

Looking at the papers on the desk and bearing in mind her complete ignorance of the business, Linda thought his request was rather a tall order, unless he intended to stay here for a considerable time.

She wanted to ask him when they'd be leaving and if she were included in the 'we' but for all his apparent charm and easy manner, there was something about her new employer that she found slightly intimidating so she remained silent.

Immediately after breakfast, which she took alone with Ronnie and Jessica the following morning, she shut herself in the office and looked rather helplessly at the pile of papers, circulars and bills lying on the desk. After sorting them vaguely, she switched on the computer and ran through the files, matching the paperwork with the material on the computer.

She was just beginning to get a glimmering of sense from it all when the door opened slowly and Jessica's small, anxious face peered round.

'Ronnie said to tell you there is coffee in the kitchen.'

Linda smiled at the child.

'There is? That's great! I could use a cup.'

Thankfully she got up and made her way to the kitchen. Only Ronnie was there, surrounded by the evidence of cooking. Two big mugs of coffee were steaming on the bench and Jessica had hauled herself up on to her favourite stool and was noisily sucking something through a straw. There was no sign of the other three adults.

'They're riding round the property,' Ronnie told her, as if in answer to her unspoken query.

'I didn't want to go,' Jessica said in a sulky voice that seemed to belie her words.

Ronnie mouthed the words, 'Wouldn't take her,' over the child's head.

At that moment, they heard the clatter of hooves. Linda took her coffee over to the window noticing as she did so that Jessica was looking thoroughly mutinous as she concentrated on sucking the last dregs, with a great deal of noise, out of her glass.

When she saw Marcia slide down off the back of a showy Palomino that had been in the yard with the other horses the day before, and throw her reins at Bluey in an arrogant gesture before she started walking to the house, Linda hastily resumed her seat at the bench.

The three in the kitchen listened in silence as the front door banged. Footsteps came up the hallway and Marcia strode into the kitchen. 'Coffee, please, Ronnie,' she demanded.

Silently, Ronnie flicked the electric jug on to reheat and made a cup of instant coffee which she placed on the bench.

'Thanks!'

Marcia's thanks were as ungracious as her please had been. Linda studied her over the rim of her coffee mug. In spite of the heat she did not look unduly hot and her face beneath the large shady felt hat was impeccably made up.

'I'll take it into the lounge. It's cooler there. I should have had more sense than to let Bluey persuade me to go out.'

She pulled off her hat and looked directly at

Linda as she spoke, almost as if she were challenging her, though what about, Linda hadn't a clue. If the woman thought she was after Bluey, then she needn't worry!

'I gather Derek has confined you to the office,' she said over her shoulder to Linda as she headed for the comparative coolness of the lounge with her coffee.

Linda, gulping down her coffee, was aware that she had been put in her place. She got down from her stool and with a brief thanks to Ronnie for the coffee, made her way back to the office. She tried not to wince at the stiffness she felt from the riding the day before. It was galling to see Marcia still elegant and cool-looking and certainly not in the least saddle sore as she had felt.

By the time she had sorted through the bills and generally straightened up the paper work in the office, there really didn't seem much more she could do on her own and she wasn't sorry when the door was pushed open cautiously and Jessica peered anxiously in.

'Hello!' Linda greeted her.

'Hello. May I come in?'

'Sure! Come along!'

Linda smiled a welcome, and Jessica stood silently by her for some minutes before asking shyly, 'Why haven't you got the computer on?'

'Well, I didn't really need to put it on for what I was doing,' Linda explained.

'Are you going to switch it on?'

Looking at the intent, little face Linda realised that this was more by way of a request than a question.

'Do you want me to?' she asked.

The child nodded.

As the computer hummed into life Jessica stared at it as if entranced.

'Can I play a game?' she asked.

As there seemed no real work to do at this point, Linda could see no harm in letting the child go into the games, and half an hour later they were both so absorbed that neither heard the door open. Both jumped guiltily at Derek's voice.

'I hope you are not hindering Linda, Jessica.'

Linda jumped to her feet, feeling like a schoolgirl caught out in some misdemeanour.

'Oh, no, not at all. Actually I've gone though the paper work and sorted things out. I didn't quite know what to do next—I mean—well, I thought you would like to go through things.'

Linda floundered to a halt.

'Oh, don't worry about all that. You can deal with that with Bluey tomorrow.'

Derek seemed to dismiss her comment with an airy wave of his hand.

'But I'm really glad to see you getting on so well with Jessica. She'll be staying here when Marcia and I go back to Melbourne this afternoon.'

The implication was quite clear. She, too, would be staying here. Linda would have asked him when she would be going to Melbourne as that was where she had expected to be when she took on this job, but suddenly it seemed preferable to be here at Bluegums with Ronnie, Bluey and Jessica than in Melbourne with Derek and Marcia. She said nothing.

'Am I staying here, Daddy?' Jessica asked.

Linda thought what a strange little thing she was and once again felt a sharp pang of pity for her. It was painfully obvious that Marcia found her a nuisance and her father didn't seem all that much better.

' 'Fraid so, pet!'

He ruffled her hair and spoke with the sympathetic tones so many adults seemed to adopt with children particularly when imposing their own will on them.

'You know you always like being with Ronnie and now you'll have Linda as well!'

'Yes,' the child said with a dead-pan expression, then with a touch of animation, 'Is it lunch time?'

'As a matter of fact, it is, which is why I'm here.'

Derek and Marcia left as soon as lunch was finished and it seemed to Linda that the house breathed a sigh of relief and settled back into its own routine.

CHAPTER THREE

Seeing the huge dog, Tarquin, stretched out on the veranda where he had been lying when she first arrived, Linda realised that she had not noticed him around for the last forty-eight hours. The thought had barely crossed her mind when Jessica ran out, dropping down beside the great animal putting her arms round his neck.

'I bet you're glad she's gone, aren't you?' she said screwing up her eyes as a huge pink tongue swept up her cheek.

Linda, who still felt a few qualms around the animals, was amazed at the child's courage.

'Do you like Tarquin?' she asked.

'He's my best friend here. He loves me. But he doesn't like Marcia. She makes Daddy keep him shut up when she is here.'

Dropping into one of the cane chairs on the veranda, Linda decided it might be diplomatic to befriend the dog. But action didn't seem called for on her part for he lumbered to his feet and padded over to her, laying his great head in her lap. She was idly caressing it when she was startled by Bluey's voice behind her.

'Made friends with the old fellow, have you?'

His voice sounded warm and friendly

though still with that hint of amusement, at her expense. Linda mumbled something about it being better to have him on her side than against her then, removing Tarquin's head from her lap with some difficulty, she scrambled to her feet.

'I've done the best I could in the office, but perhaps you could tell me what else you want doing?'

He followed her back into the house and showed her the various programmes he had on the computer to facilitate the smooth running of the farm property. He explained to her how he kept tabs on the whereabouts of all the stock and showed her how to record the movement of the cattle they had moved to another paddock the day before.

He stopped speaking and looked at her as if making a sudden decision.

'I have to go into town this afternoon. How about coming with me and getting yourself a good pair of boots and a sensible hat?'

Linda hesitated for the briefest of seconds, then agreed.

'Better ask Ronnie if she wants to come, too, or wants us to get anything.'

Bluey was already striding towards the kitchen. Linda followed in his wake.

'No, thanks,' Ronnie replied, 'but could you take Jessica?'

So it was that ten minutes later the three set off in the four-wheel drive for town which

Linda discovered was Echuca, on the Murray river, the natural border between New South Wales and Victoria.

'You'll like Echuca. Of course it is a bit touristy nowadays. Paddle steamers still ply the Murray though their cargo these days is holiday makers.'

They spent a happy couple of hours in the town. For the first hour, Bluey disappeared about his own business after steering Linda in the direction of the right shops to acquire suitable boots and hat. They then met and walked down to the river and looked at the paddle steamers.

'Can we go on one?' Jessica asked eagerly.

'Well, we should be getting back,' Bluey began, then glancing down and seeing the child's crestfallen face and following Linda's glance towards a boat just loading with passengers he made a snap decision.

'Yes, why not? Come on, girls!'

And he shepherded them before him on to the boat. It was a short but magical cruise, much enjoyed by all three as they relaxed in the holiday atmosphere. It was over all too soon.

Back at the homestead, Linda deposited her new purchases in her room then hurried to the kitchen to see if Ronnie needed any help with the evening meal. As she approached the door she heard two voices deep in earnest discussion but when she walked in both

Ronnie and Bluey stopped speaking and she found herself walking into a wall of silence. Bluey mumbled something about having to see to the horses and left the kitchen by the back door.

'I just came to see if I could help with anything,' Linda asked, feeling that she had interrupted something and maybe should have turned round and walked out so that they could continue their discussion.

'Thanks, but everything is just about ready. You could collect Jessica.'

Bluey was unusually silent over the meal. Linda found him very different company to the light-hearted companion of the afternoon who had treated them to the boat trip and appeared to enjoy it as much as Jessica and herself. Ronnie, too, seemed pre-occupied. Only the child who seemed to be getting over her initial shyness with Linda chattered happily.

Over the next few days Linda found herself cast more in the rôle of child-carer than anything else. While she liked Jessica and found her good company it was not exactly what she had expected to do when she came out to Australia. It seemed that her considerable secretarial and computer skills were not to be put to much use at all.

Bluey, it seemed, was as anxious to keep her out of the office as Derek had been to get her into it. She spent a lot of time outdoors with him and under his guidance became a much more confident horsewoman. True, good boots, comfortable jeans and a large, shady hat of her own helped. Bluey could be good company, and in spite of her avowed intent never to be taken in by a man again, Linda enjoyed their time together. She found him attractive.

One thing, however, did disturb her. It seemed that every time she came across Ronnie and Bluey together, they were deep in some discussion that very definitely excluded her. They would stop talking and either change the subject to some harmless topic or a silence would fall.

Once Linda distinctly heard her name mentioned as she was about to walk into the kitchen. She stopped in her tracks and though she didn't actually eavesdrop, she did try to hear more. But whatever it was they had been talking about it must have all been said for a silence fell.

This time Linda turned away and went out to the veranda where she found Jessica playing with Tarquin. She dropped down into one of the cane chairs. She would dearly have liked to have known what they were saying about her, and tried to comfort herself with the thought that it was probably nothing of any importance. Nevertheless an unpleasant idea took root in the back of her mind that there was something going on at Bluegums about which she knew nothing.

It was raining now, and Bluey had disappeared somewhere in the four-wheel drive. Jessica had gone off to the kitchen and was busy baking with Ronnie. Linda, feeling bored and at a loose end, made her way to the office. Browsing through the files and disks on the computer she came across one with her own name on it. Natural curiosity made her put it up on screen.

There was nothing odd about it, just her details accurately recorded as she had given them when she applied for the job. But it was the footnote that puzzled her and sent a slight prickle of apprehension running down her spine. It read, 'This one seems ideal. No close relatives.'

She could accept, happily, that her skills and eagerness to come to Australia made her an ideal candidate for the job, but why should the fact that she had no close relatives be a factor? It was, of course, quite true, and she remembered the question in the application form that had asked about parents and even brothers and sisters. She recalled it because it had seemed irrelevant at the time.

Of her biological parents she knew nothing and her adoptive parents had both been killed in a car accident when she was seventeen. With no loving grandparents and only an old aunt of her adoptive father, whom she scarcely knew, she had been very much on her own for the last five years.

Sufficient money had been left to her to give her a good training, but certainly, she thought, there could be few people who had less relations than she had. Seeing it spelled out before her on the computer screen as, apparently, of more importance than her acquired skills, engendered something of a cold chill.

She closed down the file and was just shutting down the computer when she was aware that Bluey was standing behind her in the open door of the office.

'What are you doing?' he asked coldly.

'Nothing, really,' Linda replied, finding the ready colour creeping up her throat as she met his eyes, now glacially cold.

To her annoyance she felt as guilty as a small child caught out in some misdemeanour.

'What happened to those accounts I sorted out when Derek was here?' she asked. 'I can't seem to find them.'

'I expect he took them with him to pay,' Bluey told her. 'What were you looking for on the computer?'

'Nothing in particular,' Linda replied. 'I was just trying to make myself familiar with the farm business so that I could do the office work I thought I was employed for.'

She tried not to sound too defensive but could see no need for Bluey to stand there looking at her with that accusing look in

45

his eyes.

She pulled the plastic cover over the computer screen and swivelled round on the office chair to face him.

'To tell you the truth, I am beginning to wonder what I have been employed for,' she said. 'I thought when I answered the advertisement that I was coming out to work in a city office instead of which I seem to be having a sort of extended holiday in the country!'

'Aren't you the lucky one!' he told her. 'Make the most of it while you can. If you are yearning for the city, I feel quite sure our boss will send for you sooner or later. In the meantime, well—'

He tailed off and shrugged as if he didn't quite know how to finish.

'In the meantime, you're the boss and I'm the jillaroo. Isn't that right?'

She got up and made to move past him out of the office but he caught her arm and stopped her in her tracks.

'Don't be like that, Linda.'

'Like what?'

'Truculent!'

He looked down at her and his eyes were now warm and smiling with that irrepressible twinkle lurking in their depths.

'Can't we be friends?' he asked gently.

Linda was acutely aware of his hand on her arm and of the physical nearness of him. To

46

her annoyance she could feel her pulse fluttering and was forced to lower her eyes from his face as she replied with a sarcasm she didn't really intend.

'Yes, boss! Now may I come through, please?'

She wished she could have said the same thing differently. Yes, let's be friends would have done because she did like him and did value his friendship but as she remembered Kevin and the bitter pill she had been forced to swallow when he dropped her for another woman was still too sharp in her mind.

*   *   *

Back in her own room she stood disconsolately for a few moments looking out at the rain. This was the first wet day she had experienced since coming to Australia. Give it its due, she thought glumly, when it did rain it did it in style. There seemed no such thing as moderation in this country, she decided.

Turning away from the window, she flung herself down on the bed and, picking up the book she was reading, tried to involve herself in the plight of the heroine. The poor girl was an idiot, she decided, and flung the book down in disgust to dwell instead on her own situation.

She wished Sandy was here with her, to talk things over. Then everything might seem more normal. On the heels of that thought came the inevitable, I wish I had never come!

'Come on, Linda Weston,' she admonished herself out aloud. 'Where is your famous sense of adventure?'

Truth to tell, it seemed to be buried under the uneasy feeling that had taken hold of her when she read about herself on the computer screen. Why was it so important to her new employer that she was just about alone in the world? It was a question she shied away from answering. The implications were altogether too sinister.

'Come on,' she told herself. 'You're just letting your imagination run away with you. Better stop it before you freak out altogether!'

She knew she was giving herself good advice but it was hard to take. She wished she could blot out the memory of Bluey's eyes, cold as steel as he stood there watching her. She liked Bluey, at least she had thought she did till then, and above all she wanted to trust him.

Over the next few days it seemed to Linda that Bluey went out of his way to keep her busy, away from the office. When he hadn't some job for her to do outside with him, Ronnie found something inside and between times she found herself acting as some sort of unofficial mother substitute to Jessica. She didn't really mind this for she was an easy child and was gradually coming out of her shell in Linda's company.

'Don't you go to school?' she asked the child one day.

'Yes, but it is holidays at the moment. I go back at the end of January. When is that?'

'Well, I suppose you could say next week,' Linda told her. 'It is the twenty-third today.'

The child's face immediately took on the tight, closed look Linda was getting to know. It was the look she wore when she was unhappy or bothered about something.

'Don't you like school?'

'Oh, yes. Least I don't mind it, but I shall have to go back to Melbourne. That's where school is,' Jessica explained.

'You don't like living in Melbourne?'

The small face closed up, lips tight, but she couldn't stop herself shaking her head in a definite negative. Something about the sympathetic look on Linda's face, or maybe just the fact that she didn't probe with more questions, led the child to go on.

'I don't like Marcia,' she said in a voice so soft that it could scarcely be heard.

It was on the tip of Linda's tongue to add, 'That makes two of us,' but an uncharacteristic caution made her keep silent.

It was later that evening that the phone rang. Bluey answered it and after a few moments called Linda to it.

'For me?'

'It's Derek,' Bluey told her as he handed her the receiver.

49

Even on the phone, Linda could hear what she mentally dubbed as conscious charm in his voice.

'I know you were expecting to be in Melbourne when you took this job, Linda, not buried up in the country so I'm sure you will be glad to come down to the city. I've just realised that Jessica is due to go back to school and while I am sure she would be delighted to stay up there on permanent holiday, I'm afraid that just isn't on. So I want you, if you will, to come to Melbourne with her tomorrow.'

'Yes—yes, of course,' Linda replied wondering what choice she had anyway.

'Good. I appreciate that!'

Derek made it sound as if she had a choice and was doing it to please him.

'I suggested to Bluey that he bring you down but he tells me he is very busy so he will put you both on the train. I'll meet you at Spencer Street Station. So I'll see you there at four o'clock tomorrow afternoon, or thereabouts.'

'Yes, thank you,' Linda replied.

Even as she spoke, she was wondering just what she was actually thanking him for and felt a sharp disappointment that Bluey wasn't taking them. In fact, to her dismay, it was almost as if he had delivered a physical slap for it was more than disappointment she felt, but the pain of rejection. Giving herself a mental shake she realised Derek was still on the line.

'So just wait there. Stay on the platform if I

happen to be late.'

Linda wanted to ask Bluey why he had, apparently, refused to take them by road, but somehow she couldn't bring herself to frame the words. It was he himself who broached the subject on the way to the station.

'Sorry I couldn't take you all the way, Linda.'

'Don't worry. I'm sure the train journey will be pleasant and interesting,' she told him.

Jessica, looking the picture of doomed misery, was seated between them and Linda spoke over the child's head. She herself was quite pleased at the prospect of going to Melbourne. After all that was where she had expected to be.

'Look, Linda,' he said intensely, his eyes fixed on the road ahead, 'if you need a friend, any time, if you want to talk to someone, ring me. You have the phone number of Bluegums?'

She nodded.

'Yes,' she assured him, 'I have the number.'

'And you will call me?'

She wondered at his insistence.

'Of course,' she reassured him. 'I haven't anyone else I could possibly call in Australia, have I? But why should I need to? I mean I'm not actually expecting to need to.'

'No, no, of course not. But just promise me you will, if you do need help.'

More to pacify him than anything else Linda

promised and tried to quell the niggle of anxiety that his words had brought on. Far from reassuring her they had actually alarmed her!

All too soon, the drive was over and Bluey was settling them on to the train. The call was coming over the loudspeaker for non-travellers to leave the train as it was about to depart. Suddenly, taking her quite by surprise, Bluey caught her shoulders and bent to kiss her lightly and swiftly on the lips before turning and jumping down to the platform.

'Use a call box! Reverse the charges if necessary,' he told her before leaping off the train just as it began to move.

Linda dropped down into the corner seat he had secured for her and looked across at the silent child in the corner seat opposite her, horrified to see that the big eyes were swimming with tears. With a defiant gesture, Jessica brushed them away with the back of her hand and managed a tremulous smile.

'I'm glad you are coming to Melbourne, too, Linda,' she said giving a rather shaky smile before turning her face to the window and apparently absorbing herself in the passing scenery.

Linda, with so many disturbing thoughts of her own, was too preoccupied to give much more thought to the child. Her lips still burned from the totally unexpected touch of Bluey's kiss. And what on earth did he mean with all that about phoning him if she found herself in trouble of any sort?

She wished he was here with her and she could question him further. Or did she? Wasn't his presence at times all together too disturbing, and hadn't she vowed that as far as men were concerned she just wasn't interested in them any more?

With a supreme effort of will she made herself enjoy the journey and observe the countryside they were passing through. After all she hadn't seen much of Victoria on the journey up from the airport. This time she intended to stay awake.

Jessica responded to her questions and comments and chattered happily like any normal child until they reached the outer suburbs of Melbourne when she became silent and closed up. Her small face became a mask, her feelings and thoughts locked inside.

Linda looked at her with some concern. If this was the effect that the prospect of living with her father and Marcia had on the child, she only hoped the reality would not prove too disastrous. For the first time she began to think she might possibly be glad to call Bluey after all, if only for a cheerful word.

*   *   *

The train drew into Spencer Street Station exactly on time.

53

She helped Jessica down on to the platform and piled their luggage round them as she looked round anxiously for Derek, or whoever had been detailed to meet them. As the platform cleared slowly and they were left there, she began to wonder if they had indeed been forgotten .

However at that moment Jessica cried, 'Here's Daddy!' then her voice dropping, she added, 'Oh, she's with him!'

Linda shared some of the child's feelings as she saw the tall, willowy Marcia, as usual dressed like a fashion plate, advancing along the platform at Derek's side.

As they approached she saw her place her hand with a possessive gesture on his arm and say something to him. He turned and smiled at her, taking his attention from his small daughter to do so. Linda saw the child's lips tighten in that oddly adult way she had when hurt or upset.

With a sigh, Linda bent and picked up the cases. She had a feeling that life in Melbourne wasn't going to be all plain sailing. With the luggage stowed in the boot of the silver limousine waiting outside the station and Jessica next to her in the back seat of the luxurious car, Linda settled back to take in Victoria's capital city as the car moved into the dense stream of traffic.

It took some time to get through the city proper and out to the pleasant and very upmarket suburb of Toorak where Derek drew into the courtyard of a block of flats. There were two rows of garages and well-cared for flower beds. Linda surmised, correctly, that the flat he eventually let her into after they had entered the outer door and taken the cases up in the lift a couple of flights would be as spacious, luxurious and well appointed as the surroundings. She was not disappointed.

To her surprise, a maid met them in the hallway of the flat and showed Linda to her room. It was pleasant and comfortable but with a hotel-type anonymity and quite lacking the cosy homeliness of her far less luxurious room at Bluegums. On the dressing table was an airmail envelope.

Alone in her room, she picked it up and caught her breath as she recognised Kevin's hand-writing. He must have got her address from Sandy. This address was where she had written to when she first applied for the job and was the one she had left back home with Sandy.

She held the letter in her hand for a moment before sliding her thumb under the flap and peeling it open. To her surprise it opened as easily as if it were not stuck at all. Instead of drawing the contents straight out she studied the envelope with care. It looked as if it had been opened before and re-sealed!

As she came to this conclusion she felt the same icy finger of apprehension touch her as when she had seen the footnote on the computer saying she had no relatives.

CHAPTER FOUR

Linda drew out the thin airmail paper from the envelope and skimmed through the letter, then sat down on the bed and read it through again, much more slowly.

My darling Linda, it began,

> *Please don't stop reading. I can imagine how angry you are with me and of course I deserve it. I can't expect you to believe it, yet I am hoping and praying that you will, but I know that I made a terrible mistake. Things haven't worked out with Sylvia at all. I guess because she just wasn't you! I know now, when it is probably too late, that it is you I really love. Please Linda, can't we start again? Will you come back home and we'll begin again where we left off? And this time I promise you it will be better!*

It was signed, *Yours in love and hope.*

She let the hand holding the letter drop into her lap and sat staring into space. She had to admit she was not untouched emotionally by Kevin's plea. But why on earth couldn't he have said all this before she left England and before—She stopped her thoughts at this point aware that the next one was, before she met Bluey.

The man meant nothing to her, whereas she and Kevin had been going out together for a year and engaged for six months, making plans for their wedding when he had suddenly changed his mind and in doing so changed the whole course of her life.

It wasn't Kevin's fault that she had lost her job around that time, too. The firm she worked for had gone bankrupt and that, as far as jobs for her or anyone else went, was that. Losing her job and him at the same time had, however, been a devastating disruption in her life. But Linda was always one to look for the silver lining, in this case the chance to strike out and see something of the world.

The advertisement in the paper for people prepared to go and work in Australia had seemed at the time a truly heaven-sent opportunity. She picked up the letter and read it through again. What was she thinking about! She was getting positively maudlin.

Why, here was Kevin admitting that he loved her and that life without her was empty and begging her to go back and start again. It was the very thing she had dreamed of happening all through those first terrible weeks when he had broke off their engagement. The only problem was, she wasn't sure it was what she wanted now it was offered her.

One half of her was touched and flattered, but the other half was still angry that he should have put her through so much unhappiness for nothing. Still another part of her was exulting in her freedom and the sense of adventure that coming out to Australia had brought. Once again she firmly squashed any possible hint that Bluey might have anything to do with her feelings.

She replaced the letter slowly in its envelope, once more noticing the slight crumpling round the flap. She felt again the conviction that for some reason it had been tampered with before she received it.

It was with some reluctance that she left her room and made her way in search of the other members of the household. She found them in the lounge where Marcia was presiding, literally, over the teapot which was on a small trolley at her side. Derek was standing by her about to help himself to a biscuit and Jessica was sitting demurely in an armchair that almost engulfed her. A doll was tucked under her arm and a book lay on her lap.

'Ah, there you are, Linda,' Derek said. 'I was about to send Jessica in search of you to tell you that there was a cup of tea here. I am sure you must be in need of it after the journey.'

He picked up a cup and saucer and handed it to her with that odd smile that she found so disturbing.

'Milk, sugar?'

'Milk but no sugar, thank you!'

Feeling Marcia's eyes on her, Linda

dropped her gaze from Derek as she reached out and took the cup. She carried it over to the chair next to the one Jessica was almost lost in.

'Wouldn't you like something?' she asked the child.

'Can I have a biscuit, please?' she replied, so softly Linda could barely hear her.

Putting her cup down on a small occasional table, Linda moved across to the trolley and collected the plate of biscuits to offer the child. Once again she was aware that Marcia was watching her. This time her discomfort was laced with anger. What on earth did the woman suspect her of? If it was making a play for Derek then she needn't worry. There was no way in the world she was going to fall for him!

As the days went by, Linda began to wonder more and more why she was in Australia. Her duties seemed to be more those of a mother's help, or Marcia's help, than secretarial. Each morning she supervised Jessica dressing and had breakfast with her. Usually no-one else appeared. Then she would take her to school, only a short, ten-minute walk away.

On her return to the house, Derek would be waiting for her and have a few, very few, secretarial jobs for her to do, usually nothing more than a few letters. She was then more or less free until it was time to meet Jessica from school again. Most evenings Derek and Marcia were out and she was on her own after the child was safely in bed.

She was not unhappy, or even bored, for she enjoyed just walking and exploring Melbourne all of which was, of course entirely new to her. To her relief she saw little of Marcia who seemed to spend most of her time away from the flat.

The housework was done by the maid who came in every day. She also prepared an evening meal. Linda would indeed have been lonely if it hadn't been for Jessica.

It was loneliness more than anything else that prompted her to answer Kevin's letter. But what devil urged her to hold out any hope to him she didn't know. Maybe it was just the fact that she felt he was a link with her past and one she didn't want to sever entirely.

She didn't think she had been all that encouraging until a letter came from Sandy. She was so pleased to see her friend's handwriting, the first she had had since getting to Australia, that she ripped it open quickly without too much thought. It was only in retrospect that it occurred to her that this letter, too, could have been tampered with. An examination of the flap revealed the same slight crumpling as on the letter from Kevin.

So glad, Sandy *wrote, to hear that you and Kevin are thinking of patching things up and that you will be coming back to England.*

Linda snatched up her pen and pad and immediately scribbled back.

I don't know where you got the idea from that I am making it up with Kevin, still less coming back to England. As a matter of fact I love it here and think I shall stay, probably for ever!

As she sat alone in the lounge afterwards watching a singularly dreary TV programme, the phone shrilled through the flat. Welcoming the interruption she got up to answer it and was more pleased than she would have liked to admit to hear Bluey's voice.

'Derek isn't here,' she told him.

'Good, I don't want him. It's you I've rung up.'

'Oh!'

'How are things going, Linda?'

'OK, I suppose.'

'You don't sound too sure? Everything is all right, isn't it?'

'Yes, of course. It's just that, well, I really don't seem to have anything much to do and I wonder why I'm here at all. There is less to do here than there was at Bluegums.'

She was suddenly assailed with a wave of nostalgia for the farm homestead, for the horses, for Tarquin, for Ronnie and, yes, she had to admit it, for Bluey!

'How is everything and everyone there?' she asked, unaware of the wistful note that had crept into her voice.

'Plugging along,' he assured. 'I thought you would ring me. I asked you to.'

'Did you?'

She had thought that he had just meant her to ring if she hit problems.

'Is everything really OK with you, Linda?'

'Yes, of course. Why on earth shouldn't it be? Just one thing . . .'

She tailed off. She had been about to tell him that she was sure her letters were being opened and read before she got them, but it seemed such a trivial complaint that she decided to say nothing. But he was not going to let it go.

'What, Linda? There is something worrying you. What is it?'

She still hesitated. It did sound such a ridiculous thing and she had no proof at all.

'What, Linda? No matter how trivial you think it is, tell me.'

There was a note of authority in his voice that she automatically responded to in spite of herself.

'Well, it's my letters. I've only actually had a couple since I've been here, and it seems to me as if they have been opened and re-sealed before I get them. I'm sure I must be imagining it. What on earth would anyone want to do that for?'

'What was in the letters?'

Linda bridled slightly.

'Nothing of any importance to anyone but me. They were just private letters from friends.'

'Look, I'm not prying into your private affairs. I don't care a stuff about that. I just wondered if there was anything in them at all that could possibly have been of the slightest interest to anyone else.'

'No,' she told him shortly.

'Can you do something for me?' he asked.

'What?' she answered shortly and rather ungraciously.

'I want you to call me in a couple of days, preferably from a call box. You can reverse the charges. Tell me if anything else like that has happened. Also if there are any visitors to the flat.'

She was about to protest that her job wasn't spying on her employer and put the phone down when he added softly, 'But most of all I want to know that you are all right.'

After she had replaced the receiver she recalled their conversation in its entirety. If Bluey had meant to reassure her in any way then he had failed miserably for his obvious concern only served to fuel a latent anxiety she felt about this job and her employer.

The following morning she returned to the flat earlier than usual after taking Jessica to school as black thunder clouds had rolled up and the air was so heavy and humid that she was quite unable to summon the energy to walk anywhere.

When she walked into the flat she heard voices coming from the lounge. What caught her attention was the fact that it was not the even babble of general conversation but the sharp, staccato sentences of people in angry disagreement.

As she walked through the hallway heading for her own room, Marcia appeared in the doorway of the lounge. She stared at Linda in an odd sort of way as if she was the last person she expected to see. She opened her mouth as if about to say something then snapped it shut a second before she closed the door sharply, leaving Linda feeling as if she had received a physical slap.

In the privacy of her own bedroom, she dropped into a chair, just as there was a loud clap of thunder and the heavens opened to pour a heavy, but brief, shower on to the dusty city. As suddenly as the rain had started it stopped again and a bright, if watery, sun appeared as the clouds rolled away.

Linda got up from her chair and moved over to the window which overlooked the street. As she did so a taxi drew into the kerb and the front door to the flats opened to reveal a well-dressed man in a business suit hurrying out to it, carrying a briefcase.

While she was sure she had never actually met him, there was something about his back that was familiar. Searching her memory Linda suddenly recalled seeing him outside Jessica's school one afternoon. He had hurried away as she arrived to meet the child. The thought crossed her mind now that he had hurried away because she had arrived!

She told herself she was being fanciful, collected her umbrella and decided on a walk in the park to clear her thoughts. The more she walked, however, the more troubled she became. She felt there was something else she should be recalling but could not think what it was. When she saw a phone box, she found herself pulling the door open and going inside.

'Ronnie, hi!' she said a little breathlessly when the phone at Bluegums was answered. 'Is Bluey there?'

'No, sorry. Oh, wait, here he is, coming in for morning tea. I'll put you on.'

'Linda? Is everything all right?'

The concern in his voice was gratifying, she thought.

'I don't really know. I'm probably imagining things, but it's just that there's this man . . . I've seen him twice now, once at the flat and the other time he was outside Jessica's school. I'm pretty sure it was the same one.'

'Did you get a good look at him?'

'Well, no,' she had to admit. 'To tell the truth I didn't really see his face at all.' She tailed off thinking that it sounded very weak when put into words. 'But I'm sure it was the same person. I can't explain it. Call it gut feeling, but I was worried.'

There was a pause, and when he spoke his voice was calm and soothing.

'Yes, I can see it has alarmed you, but don't worry. Maybe it wasn't the same person after all. If you didn't actually see his face either time you can't be sure.'

Linda felt annoyed, with herself, and angry. She felt Bluey had made a fool of her. He was the one who had got her worried and made her promise to ring him if anything concerned her. Now, when she had, he wasn't taking her seriously.

'Sorry to have bothered you. I have to go now. Goodbye!'

She turned and pushed her way quickly out of the call box. She wasn't to know that at Bluegums, Bluey was turning to Ronnie with the phone still in his hands. He shrugged with exasperation.

'Dammit, Ronnie, I made a mess of that, didn't I? I wanted to soothe her down and I overdid it so I very much doubt if she will call me again if she has anything to report!'

'I'm worried about Jessica,' Ronnie said, 'and of course Linda, too. Do you think . . .'

'Yes,' Bluey cut in, 'I do. I shall have to think up a good reason to go down to Melbourne in the not too distant future.'

Blissfully unaware of their conversation, and equally unaware that she was being watched, Linda made a snap decision to board a city-bound tram that had just halted at the stop close by. There was time to go shopping before she was due to collect Jessica from school.

67

In one of the big shopping malls she headed for a department store. One of the things she had had little chance to do since she came to Australia was wander round a large store. Though she enjoyed herself, she soon decided that big stores, like big hotels, were really not that much different whether in London or Melbourne.

Treating herself to a coffee, she began to think wistfully of Bluegums. Now that had been different to anything she had experienced before. But thinking about the farm brought Bluey to mind and at the moment he was the last person she wanted to think about!

Glancing at her watch, she realised it was time she was moving or she would be late meeting Jessica at school. Her conscience reminded her that she had few enough duties in this strange situation she had landed herself in so she had better fulfil those she had to the best of her ability.

To her dismay, school was out when she arrived at the gates and she couldn't see any sign of Jessica. Suppose she hadn't been imagining things and that man had been waiting at the school with some sinister intent, like kidnapping Jessica! To her immense relief, however, she heard her name called and saw a small figure detach itself from a group of children and come running towards her.

'Oh, Jessica! Thank goodness!' she cried in relief.

'I was waiting for you,' the child told her solemnly.

When they got back to the flat, Derek and Marcia were having afternoon tea in the lounge. Linda's first inclination was to take herself off to her own room but as she made her way towards it her employer called her to join them. Marcia was lolling back in an armchair tapping her long nails lightly on the arm and managing to look supremely bored.

Derek was chatting to Jessica about her school and friends. It all seemed cosy and harmless enough until Jessica unwittingly told Derek that Linda had been late.

'While I was waiting for Linda—'

She tailed off, suddenly conscious that in some way she had said the wrong thing as Derek cut in sharply.

'What do you mean, Jessica? Isn't Linda always there when you come out of school?'

'Yes, only today she was a teeny bit late.'

The child looked hastily from her father to Linda. Across the room, Marcia raised her eyebrows in a gesture that spoke volumes.

'Is that correct? Were you late?' Derek asked Linda.

'Well, yes, but as Jessica said, it was only a few minutes.'

'A few minutes late could be too late!' Derek cut in making Linda colour and begin to apologise and make excuses for herself.

'I'm sorry. It took me longer to get there

from the town centre than I thought. I'll try not to let it happen again.'

'You will not let it happen again, if you please! It is most important that you are there—waiting—when Jessica comes out of school.'

Linda felt very much like a naughty schoolgirl hauled up in front of the class for a public dressing-down. Jessica was looking troubled, aware that somehow she had managed to precipitate this and across the room Marcia was obviously enjoying every second, which added considerably to Linda's discomfort. True she was at fault, but she could not see she had committed such a crime. Jessica was here safe and sound, so no harm had been done.

'I'm sorry,' she repeated, adding as he gestured to the teapot, 'No, thanks. I won't have any tea.'

She turned on her heel and made for her room feeling really cross with herself.

In the seclusion of her own room she calmed down and asked herself just why she felt so angry. After all she was in the wrong, but surely not so much in the wrong that she needed to be reprimanded like a naughty child, and in front of Marcia, too!

She thought of Bluey, and this was not soothing either. He had dismissed her anxiety. What was the matter with everyone, for goodness' sake? It seemed to her that they either belittled every worry she had or made worries where none really existed. She was tired of it all.

She just wanted things to be straightforward and normal, and she would like to have a straightforward, normal office job without any emotional tangles—the sort of job she thought she was coming to when she first came out to Australia!

It was while her thoughts were jumping all over the place that her eye caught the letter from Kevin lying where she had let it fall on the dressing table. She picked it up and began to read it again, walking over to the window and dropping down into the one comfortable chair the room boasted.

As when she first read it the words were balm to her bruised spirit. Maybe it really would be better to take him up on his offer and go back to England and start again where they had left off. After all, they had had a pretty good relationship for two years and she knew Kevin in a way she certainly did not know anyone here.

By the time she had read through the letter twice she had just about talked herself back into being in love with him again. She had certainly almost decided to write to him and take up his offer. She decided to wait until after dinner.

Often Derek and Marcia were out for the evening meal and Linda and Jessica were left to themselves but tonight they remained in and the four of them sat down round the dining table. Linda wondered idly if Marcia could perform any domestic chores at all. Certainly she had never yet seen her do anything more arduous than pour a drink, and tonight's meal had been prepared by the maid before she left.

Derek seemed determined to make amends for his curtness earlier on and went out of his way to be pleasant, even charming, something which it was obvious Marcia thought quite unnecessary. Linda would have remained silent but he kept drawing her into the conversation.

In spite of herself, she had to admit that when he tried to be pleasant he could be charming indeed, and tonight he was making a real effort. He chatted to Jessica, drawing the child out so that she became quite animated.

'I hope you have remembered we are going to the theatre tonight,' Marcia cut into the conversation, addressing herself to Derek.

He looked at his watch.

'Yes, of course, I have. It doesn't start until eight o' clock and it is barely seven now. We had dinner early.'

'Well, I'm going to get ready. I don't want any coffee.'

Marcia got up from the table and walked out of the room.

'Would you like coffee?' Linda asked Derek.

'I think I have time for a small one,' he replied.

He smiled at her across the table as she, too, got up and headed to the kitchen to bring in the pot which was gently percolating.

'Can I leave the table?' Jessica asked.

Linda looked across at Derek, unwilling to be the one who made the decision in her father's presence. But he nodded.

'By all means, trot along.'

Linda felt suddenly ill at ease as she realised that she and Derek were alone. As she passed him his coffee, their fingers touched and she was sure it was not accidental.

'Linda,' he said slowly looking across the table at her as he thoughtfully stirred his coffee, 'I really am sorry if I seemed a bit sharp with you. It's just that, well, I do worry about Jessica, you know. I wouldn't like anything to happen to her!'

'Yes, I quite understand,' she replied stiffly.

He bestowed on her that charming smile of his, a smile which, in spite of herself, made Linda very aware of him as a man.

'Let's forget it then. I'm sure you will be more careful in the future,' he said, glancing at his watch. 'I suppose I had better spruce myself up a little for going to the theatre.'

Linda rose from the table and began to gather up the dishes. She always cleared up in the evening. It went against the grain for her to leave everything for the maid to do in the morning. As she reached across to pick up his coffee cup, Derek caught her by the arm. Sheer surprise as much as his physical grip made her freeze in her tracks.

'You are a most attractive girl, but I suppose you know that. I'm sure you have been told so many times.'

Linda didn't quite know how it happened but somehow he was on his feet and she had put the coffee cup down again and he was drawing her to him. His lips were moving towards hers. Whether she would have responded to him or not she never found out, for at that moment Marcia's voice said coldly from the doorway, 'Are you ready, Derek?'

CHAPTER FIVE

Linda grabbed up the tray and, clattering china on it, hurried out to the kitchen uncomfortably aware of the flush spreading up her neck and into her cheeks.

She rinsed the plates furiously under the hot tap before stacking them in the dishwasher. Subconsciously, she strained her ears to catch what Marcia was saying, but all she could hear was a tinkling laugh which somehow, she felt sure, was directed at her.

She closed the dishwasher and made her way to supervise Jessica's bath. Jessica was still in the bath when they left. Derek stuck his head round the door and bade them both a brief good-night. He must have suggested that Marcia did the same for Linda heard her say, 'No, I don't want to get splashed.'

The child heard, too, for Linda saw her small face close up in that way she had that was more expressive than any complaint. As the outer door of the flat closed behind them she turned to Linda.

'I don't like Marcia, do you?'

While Linda was still thinking of an answer that would be truthful yet still bear repetition, Jessica added, 'I don't mind Daddy, but I like Bluey better, don't you?'

Mercifully she continued without waiting

for a reply.

'But best of all I like Mummy. I wish I could be with her all the time.'

This was the first time Linda had heard a mother mentioned. Somehow it hadn't occurred to her that one was still in the picture, which she supposed was foolish, for in today's social climate it was far more likely that Derek was divorced than a widower. She would have liked to question the child further but Jessica closed up on her now and began talking about school.

Once the child was safely tucked up in bed Linda made her way to the lounge and flicked on the TV. She sat for a while idly changing channels. Nothing caught her attention enough to continue watching it and her thoughts wandered again to Kevin and his letter. She wondered if he really meant what he said, and what had prompted him to say it. Well, at least if she wrote to him she could find out a bit more and who knew where it could lead?

She had barely made the decision and was about to collect writing materials when the phone interrupted her thoughts. She was surprised to hear Bluey's voice after their last telephone conversation.

'Oh, hello,' she said stiffly.

She nearly added that she didn't think he would want to talk to her again but decided that sounded too childish and besides she didn't even know if it was her he wanted to talk to. He was probably ringing to discuss farm business with Derek.

'You all right, Linda?' he asked, and she warmed at the note of anxiety in his voice. 'I thought you sounded a bit rattled when I was talking to you before. I was a bit worried.'

'Oh, everything is fine, just fine!' she insisted, quelling the small voice that insisted that this was not strictly true.

'Good, and Jessica? Is she OK?'

'Of course, why shouldn't she be?'

The wild thought crossed Linda's mind that he, as well as Derek, was anxious about the child. It was on the tip of her tongue to tell him what had happened that day, but after all, what had happened? There was really nothing to tell, only that she had received a reprimand. She decided to keep quiet.

It was only after she had replaced the phone that it crossed Linda's mind to wonder where Bluey was calling from. She was getting too whimsical altogether. Of course Bluey was at Bluegums. Why should she think that he might be in Melbourne, and wouldn't he have told her if he was?

She decided that she was letting her imagination run away with her. It must be the result of having too little to do. She would answer Kevin's letter, now. But what to say was another matter. Somehow the sound of Bluey's voice on the phone had made going

77

back to Kevin less attractive. What was she talking about? Neither of them meant anything to her—anything at all. She was a free spirit and that she intended to remain.

In the end she went to bed with the radio on in her room and a half-written letter to Kevin on the pad. When she had started to write she didn't know what to say to him. One part of her longed to take up where they had left off, another wanted only to be free. She finally hedged her bets by writing a friendly but quite noncommittal note which she hoped would keep the lines open without making any promises.

Sleep, she found, did not come easily that night. When she did drop off she was roused by Jessica having a nightmare and calling out in her dream. She couldn't hear the exact words but it sounded something like, 'No, leave me alone. No, I don't want to come with you.'

When she asked the child about her nightmare she either couldn't or wouldn't tell her. Linda administered hot milk and soothing words and finally padded back to her own bed where she lay awake, wondering.

Tonight had been the first time Jessica had ever mentioned her mother. That the child was fond of her father was obvious and it was equally clear that she hated Marcia. Linda was sympathetic here. She had noticed how fond Jessica and Ronnie appeared of one another

78

when they were all at Bluegums, the child often preferring to stay in the kitchen rather than go out on the farm property, even riding with them.

*　　*　　*

When she heard no more of Bluey in the next few days, Linda decided she must have been letting an overwrought imagination run riot to think he was actually in Melbourne. As for herself she was afraid to go too far afield again in case she was unwittingly late to pick up Jessica from school and this time there was some disaster.

Derek suddenly seemed to require a lot more office work from her, too. As some of it seemed trivial and almost unnecessary, Linda wondered how genuine and urgent it really was or whether it was a ploy to keep her anchored at base.

Derek himself spent a lot more time in the flat. Where Marcia went, Linda neither knew nor asked. Sometimes he would be in the office dictating letters to her or getting her to do something on the computer for him; at others he would be receiving a steady stream of people. Some of these he saw in the lounge and some in the office. On these occasions he always made it clear that he did not want Linda around.

In spite of herself she had to admit he was

79

attractive and, in his treatment of her, charming and courteous if, at times, more forthcoming than she would have liked.

'Yes?'

She swivelled round to face him on the office chair, waiting for the next sentence of the letter he was dictating to her.

'What next?'

'What next indeed? I was just thinking how very attractive you are, Linda.'

He smiled into her eyes as he spoke. She felt the ready warmth creeping up her neck, to her annoyance, and then dropped her eyes to the keyboard.

'What next, in the letter?' she repeated pointedly.

'The letter? Oh, yes, I was thinking of other things. What are you planning to do next, Linda?'

'Next? I don't know. I suppose that depends on you.'

She felt confused and not at all sure just what he was getting at.

'I mean, what are your plans for the future? Do you plan to stay in Australia for ever? Haven't you got a boyfriend back home in England? I'm sure you must have, a pretty girl like you!'

Linda glanced at him in some confusion. He was looking at her so strangely. She wasn't at all sure whether he was making a pass at her, suggesting she go back to England or even threatening her. As if he could see these thoughts flitting through her mind, or maybe he read them from her face, he leaned over and put his hand on her knee.

'It's a pity I am so tied up with Marcia, but she is very busy at the moment . . .'

He tailed off and Linda was left to use her imagination about his real meaning for at that moment the door bell shrilled and he immediately stood up.

'Ah, my dear, I'm afraid I have an appointment, if you will excuse me. No need to bother any more with that letter. If you want to go out for a breath of fresh air, feel free to do so.'

She was clearly dismissed. As she crossed the lobby on her way out she heard raised voices coming from the lounge. She paused for a second, not listening but definitely taking in. The voice she heard raised was a strange one and now Derek was answering and his voice was low, utterly controlled and threatening.

Linda felt a shiver run down her spine in spite of the warmth of the summer day. Suddenly she was afraid. What sort of people were these she had got involved with? She hurried out, anxious to be away from the flat which seemed to have taken on a sinister, almost threatening atmosphere.

In spite of the sun and the warmth outside, she shivered and, needing to be with other people, headed for a small café she knew where she could sit on the pavement and watch the world go by and have a long cool drink or a reviving cup of coffee.

As she hurried along she was beset by the uneasy feeling that someone was following her, but, turning round, she couldn't see anyone in particular, though of course there were other people, but all seemed intent on their own business.

Nevertheless, she could not rid herself of this uncomfortable feeling. She tried an old trick, stopping to look in a shop window, while in actual fact her focus was on the reflection of the street and pavement in the glass. She saw a young man stop to light a cigarette. That must be the one, she decided, and failed to notice the attractive, young woman admiring the goods in the next window.

The café was crowded, with most of the outdoor tables full. She found a small one for two and noticed the young man join a group at another table. She relaxed. He probably wasn't interested in her at all. When an attractive girl, a little older than herself, asked if she could share her table she agreed readily with only a vague feeling that she had seen her somewhere before.

'Thanks a lot!'

The newcomer smiled as she dropped thankfully into the seat opposite Linda. She pushed her sunglasses on to the top of her head and peered at her.

'I've seen you before, I'm sure I have!'

'Funny you saying that, because I thought the same about you when you first came up to me,' Linda agreed.

At that moment, the waitress came up and both girls ordered coffee then resumed their conversation, wondering where they could have met. Suddenly her companion snapped her fingers, making Linda jump.

'I know,' she said triumphantly. 'It was on the plane! You came out from England last month, right?'

'Right!' Linda agreed. 'We must have seen one another on the plane. Are you English or Australian?'

'I'm neither, or both, whichever way you look at it. English by birth, but came out here when I was six years old and now Australian by nationality. But I have been in England for the last two years on an extended working holiday. How about you?'

'I'm doing it the other way round. I've come out here to a job. But to tell you the truth a lot of it has seemed like a holiday.'

Linda found herself telling her new friend about her job and how little work she really seemed asked to do.

'I thought I was going to do office work, but there seems so little that I don't really know why they employ me. Of course, I am useful, I suppose, looking after the little girl. But that isn't what I came here for you. Mind you, she is a nice kid. Funny thing is I came out to work in a city and was pretty fed up when I found myself on a farm, yet in the end that was what I really enjoyed and I miss it.'

'I guess once you get to know the Australian bush you will always miss it when you go somewhere else. I know I do. I was brought up on a farm.'

There was a wistful note in the other girl's voice but she soon shrugged off her nostalgia.

'Mind you, I love Melbourne.'

Linda discovered her name was Jane Foster. They exchanged phone numbers and agreed to meet if possible round about the same time the next day.

'If I don't turn up you'll know I am on the computer, at last!' Linda told her. 'But I'll try and give you a call if I can't make it.'

It was only after they had parted and Linda was walking back that she realised that she had told Jane a lot about herself and her job and actually learned very little in return.

Oh, well, she thought, I expect I'll find out in due course, and she mentally shrugged off any concern she might have felt.

Had she seen Jane whipping a mobile phone out of her bag the moment she was out of sight and dialling hastily with a preoccupied look on her face Linda might not have felt quite so happy about her new friend.

Linda was in good time to collect Jessica from school and neither Derek nor Marcia put in an appearance for the rest of the day at the flat. The time passed peacefully and without incident. Linda noticed how much more relaxed Jessica was when they were on their own. She was also, it seemed, learning to trust her for she opened up a little more each day.

They were reading one of her favourite books in bed that night and as she closed it, almost reverently, the child said, 'My mummy used to read that to me.'

As always, when Jessica mentioned her mother, Linda was at a slight loss, not knowing whether it was best to talk about her or try and steer the conversation into safer waters. As always, the thought of her mother seemed a traumatic one. As she spoke the child's eyes were filling with tears.

She didn't know whether the programmes on the TV were particularly poor that evening or if her powers of concentration were low but after surfing through all the channels she decided to make an early night of it and go to bed with a book. But the book failed to hold her attention, too. So much seemed to have happened during the day. Some of it disturbing but her meeting with Jane made up.

Her thoughts turned to Kevin. Had she mailed the letter she had written to him? She had no recollection of doing so. She went through her pockets and looked in her shoulder bag but couldn't find it. Just as she was satisfied that she must have posted it, and was unable to recall doing so, she saw it lying on the dressing table. She picked it up and was about to stuff it in her bag when something about it caught her attention.

The seal did not seem to be sitting flat; in fact it looked just the same as her in-coming letters had. Was someone tampering with her mail both to and from England? The thought made her so angry that she almost tore the letter to shreds, but on second thoughts decided to put it in her bag and mail it the following day.

How she longed to have someone she could trust. Everyone seemed to take on a sinister look, and Linda couldn't rid herself of the thought that, beneath the surface, something about her whole set-up here in Australia wasn't all it seemed. Whom could she trust here?

Bluey's face immediately came to mind. Surely she could rely on him? Yet at times even he had behaved in what she could only describe as an odd way. She remembered the times when she suspected he and Ronnie had been discussing her. Ronnie was someone she would instinctively have trusted if it hadn't been for that very same thing.

Derek she didn't trust, as least she didn't think she did, however charming he was and as for Marcia, well! Now Jane had come on the scene and she didn't know what to think about her. She liked her and hoped she could trust her but the truth of the matter was that she had become suspicious of everything and everybody.

Oh, Sandy, Sandy, she thought longingly of her friend back in England. How I wish you were here or at least near enough to pick up the phone and talk to. She hardly felt justified in using her employer's phone to call across the world, apart from the fact that she was darned if she could work out the time difference so that she could be sure of catching Sandy!

When she finally switched off the light she felt not one whit better. Her thoughts had just gone round and round in circles till she ended up where she started, wishing that her friend was here with her, or alternatively that she had never come herself!

She woke from a troubled sleep in which she dreamed that she was being chased through a maze by someone she didn't know. She could hear the sound of raised voices then suddenly over and above this the scream of a child—Jessica!

Without stopping to think, she made for the child's bedroom which, fortunately, was next to hers.

Jessica was sitting up in bed, still flushed from sleep. Her eyes were looking round the room wildly as if she didn't know where she was when Linda switched the light on.

'Mummy!' she cried and began to sob.

Linda was at her bed in one stride and her arms were round her in a comforting hug.

'Hush!' she said. 'It's OK now!'

From the lounge room came the sound of the angry voices. It was, Linda assumed, Derek and Marcia engaged in a domestic, of some proportions by the sound of it for no-one seemed to have heard the child's scream. Jessica was now clinging to her, sobbing as if her small heart would break.

'Don't leave me, Linda,' she begged. 'I'm frightened. I thought someone was in my room.'

'You had a bad dream. You'll be all right now.'

Linda soothed her and tried to disentangle the small arms that had a monkey-like grip round her neck.

'No, it wasn't a dream. I saw someone, I know I did!' the child insisted.

As her panic didn't seem to be abating nor her hold on Linda loosening, she said soothingly, 'Look, Jessica, suppose you come into my room and get into my bed for a bit? I've got a big double bed you know, so there will be plenty of room.'

The sobbing stopped as Jessica nodded. Without more ado, Linda carried her into her own room and dropped her down on the empty side of the bed then clambered in beside her.

'There, how about that?'

'Good! Can I stay here all night?'

Linda looked at her small bedside clock—it was already three o'clock in the morning. She nodded.

'I don't see why not,' she replied, 'but I'm quite sure it was only a horrid dream you had.'

Once again Jessica shook her head and vehemently denied this.

'I was awake,' she insisted, 'and there was a man in my room!'

Rather to her surprise, Linda not only slept well for the rest of the night but slept late, and had quite a rush to get Jessica up and ready for school. The flat seemed quiet. Either no-one else was there or they hadn't got up. She met the daily maid on the doorstep as they left hurriedly for school.

After seeing the child disappear safely into the school building, Linda strolled back, enjoying the relative cool of the morning though the sun was already getting hot. As she walked, she found herself hoping she would see Jane again that afternoon and with the thought came the sharp realisation that she was really very lonely.

There just was no-one to talk to. Tina, the maid, was totally uncommunicative. To every comment or query Linda made to her she answered only with a monosyllable though at times Linda caught her glance and she would give a hesitant friendly smile before quickly turning away.

Only as she walked back into the flat and greeted the maid to get the customary non-answer did it occur to Linda that she might have been instructed not to talk.

She was just making her way to her room when Derek came out into the hallway with a sheaf of papers in his hand. He looked at her in a manner she could only think of as distraught.

'Ah, Linda. Could you come into the office for a moment?'

She followed him into the small room where the computer and filing cabinet stood and which was termed the office though in truth it was little more than a cubbyhole and not to be compared with the comfortable little office at Bluegums.

'Could you do these few letters and leave them here for me to sign? If I am not back before you need to go to fetch Jessica from school, just leave them on my desk.'

Linda looked at the pile of papers and inwardly groaned. Unless she got her skates on it was unlikely she would have time to meet Jane.

'Yes, of course,' was all she said as she sat down immediately in front of the computer and switched it on. When she actually got down to work she found that some of the letters, hastily scribbled out for her to copy, were actually identical, only the names had to be changed, so she was able to get through them more quickly than she first thought.

She was about halfway through when she heard the door bang and guessed that was Derek leaving. A short time later she heard Marcia talking to Tina in her usual high-handed manner.

Then she heard the door bang again. She gave an unconscious sigh of relief knowing that apart from Tina she was now alone in the flat. Quickly she finished the letters and after doing the envelopes left them in a neat pile, as requested, for Derek to sign.

In the kitchen she found Tina relaxing over a cup of coffee.

'You like some?' she asked, again with that fleeting smile.

'Please,' Linda replied.

'Something to eat?' Tina queried.

Linda looked up from the coffee she was stirring thoughtfully and realising that she was, in fact, quite hungry, nodded again.

'Yes, I would, please.'

Tina quickly made a plate of sandwiches which she put on the table between them. She pushed the plate towards Linda before taking one herself, without a word but with that deprecating half-smile. Surprisingly the silence between them today was comfortable rather than strained. Linda, lost in her thoughts and enjoying the sandwich almost jumped when Tina spoke.

'It is good you are here. You are kind to the

little one,' she said.

'I like her. I'm sorry for her, too,' Linda replied.

She looked across at the other woman suddenly longing to ask questions but wondering, as she found herself doing all the time these days, whether or not she could trust her. She was still wondering when Tina spoke again.

'She is a good child, in a bad place,' she said enigmatically. 'It is as well she has you to take care of her.'

It seemed to Linda that she stressed the bit about taking care of her and she would have asked more but Tina got up and walked over to the sink with her empty plate and coffee cup. There was something about her manner that said very definitely that she had said all she intended to say. Yet Linda felt there was a good deal more she knew.

CHAPTER SIX

Thanking her for the lunch, Linda headed for her room to grab a sunhat, glasses and her purse and make her way to the coffee bar in the hope that Jane would turn up. She searched the crowded tables but there was no sign of her so she decided to take a seat at a small table for two and hope she might turn up.

She had barely sat down and was debating on the relative merits of a soft drink or an ice cream to while away the time and also give her a reason for occupying a table when she heard a voice behind her.

'Hello, Linda!'

She spun round to find herself looking up into two vivid blue eyes under a thatch of hair only partially concealed beneath a wide-brimmed hat.

'Bluey!' she exclaimed, thankful for her own hat and the sunglasses, both of which she hoped would conceal a little of her pleased confusion at seeing him there.

She could feel the ready blush creeping up her neck and throat and was annoyed with herself for letting this man cause this reaction in her.

'What on earth are you doing here?' she demanded. 'Anyway, how did you know I was here, or was it just coincidence?'

Aware that she was gabbling for the sake of it she gestured towards the empty chair and somewhat ungraciously added, 'Well, sit down!'

Bluey sat, and grinned at her in that maddening way of his, maddening because for some odd reason it always made her pulse race.

'I came to see you, and how did I know where to find you? Well, Jane told me of course,' he said as if it was the most matter-of-fact explanation in the world.

'Oh!' was all Linda could think of in reply.

'Have you ordered anything?' Bluey now asked.

She shook her head.

'I couldn't decide between a soft drink and an ice cream,' she told him, wondering why on earth they were indulging in such a banal conversation.

'Be a devil, have an ice!'

'If you insist!'

She matched his teasing tone and smiled back at him feeling more lighthearted than she had for many a day. She studied his back as he went and fetched the ice-creams. When he wasn't looking directly at her with those bright, laughing eyes and was a reasonable distance off she could think about him calmly— well, more or less! He hadn't, she realised, answered her question about why he was here,

94

or how he knew Jane.

By the time he rejoined her and placed an enormous dish of ice cream in front of her, Linda's mind was churning with the many questions she wanted answers to. For the moment, though, she was content to sit in the sun, eat ice-cream and enjoy Bluey's company.

She did this so well that it was sometime before she realised that she was being quizzed, skilfully, about Derek, Marcia, even Tina and the daily happenings and comings and goings at the flat.

'Look, Bluey, I can't tell you anything because I don't know anything. Well, if you told me just what you were looking for, what you wanted to know, then it's possible I just might be a bit more help. But what about you? You haven't told me anything. What are you doing in Melbourne for instance?'

He leaned back in his chair and grinned at her.

'Eating ice cream with you.'

'Oh, Bluey, you know perfectly well what I mean.' Linda was exasperated. 'What are you here in Melbourne for, not just what you are doing at this moment.'

'Having a little holiday. Does that satisfy you?'

'Not entirely. But if it is all you are going to tell me I suppose it will have to do.'

Bluey nodded, and that seemed to be all he was going to say.

'Well, here's another one. How did you know where to find me?' she persisted.

'I thought I had answered that one already. Jane told me.'

'Yes, Bluey, but how do you know Jane, and was it an accident she met up with me the first time?'

'I've known Jane for a long time. She is a very good friend of mine, and, no, it wasn't quite by accident. Now you have the answers to your questions, how about answering a few of mine?'

Linda was not entirely satisfied, and to add to her dissatisfaction was a prickle of jealousy, when Bluey talked about his longstanding friendship with Jane. He leaned his arms on the table between them and looked at her earnestly.

'I want you to think, Linda, tell me anything that has happened since you have been here that seems in any way odd to you.'

Linda found herself automatically leaning back in her chair almost as if Bluey were threatening her, which was absurd of course, wasn't it? But the bright blue eyes had lost their laughter now and seemed to bore right into her as if challenging her to remember, and tell. She felt on the defensive and vaguely threatened.

'Well,' she began doubtfully, 'there is one thing that puzzles me and, to tell the truth, it troubles me as well. What on earth have I really been brought out here for? It's certainly not for my office and computer skills for I hardly use them. About the only thing I do is look after Jessica, something which I am sure just about anyone could do, including Tina, or even Marcia if it comes to that.'

'What you say is probably true,' Bluey conceded, 'but don't belittle what you are doing. Looking after Jessica is very important, and I am sure you do it very well. But what about the people who come to the flat, Derek's visitors? Is there anything you can tell me about them?'

'Not really.' Linda paused to think. 'The most obvious thing about them is that Derek doesn't seem to want me to know much about them. He usually has them when I am not there or despatches me to the office or something.'

'Well, what about Marcia?'

He had observed the offhand manner in which Marcia habitually treated Linda and seen her reaction. Knowing that there was no love lost between them, Bluey felt he might get some information here from Linda.

'What about her?' Linda retaliated coldly. 'We see as little as possible of each other. That's about all I can tell you.'

'And the maid—what's her name?'

'She seems nice enough, not very communicative. Comes, does her job and goes, mostly.'

Linda was getting tired of this cross examination which seemed to have no purpose and no meaning. She glanced at her watch.

'Heavens!' she exclaimed. 'Just look at the time. I shall have to dash and meet Jessica out of school!'

To her surprise Bluey instantly leaped to his feet.

'You mustn't be late!' he exhorted her, holding out his hand. 'Goodbye, Linda, I'll see you around.'

She took his hand briefly in hers.

' 'Bye, Bluey. Won't you come with me?'

He dropped her hand as if it stung.

'I think not—sorry!' and he began to turn away, then as if remembering something, he turned back. 'By the way, no need to mention to anyone that you met me, understand?'

She didn't, but even as she thought that, he disappeared among the crowds passing by on the pavement. Feeling curiously deflated, Linda gathered up her belongings and made as much haste as she could in the direction of Jessica's school.

Jessica was one of the last to come out and Linda was beginning to get anxious when to her relief she saw her making her way towards her. Trustingly the child slipped her hand into hers and she felt a warm glow. This was the first time she had done this of her own volition and Linda was glad to think that she was now accepted as a friend.

She guessed that the incident of the bad dream had much to do with it. But Jessica was still not prepared to admit that it had been a dream as Linda discovered when she tucked her into bed that night and attempted to bid her good-night.

As she would have moved away from the bed two thin, but surprisingly strong, little arms suddenly locked themselves round her own arm.

'Don't go, Linda, please!' Jessica begged. 'I'm scared!'

'Scared? What of?' she asked, making her voice as light and casual as she could.

'Someone might come into my room again.'

'But, Jessica, I told you, that was just a bad dream. No-one was in your room. How could they be? They couldn't get in through your window, and they couldn't get into the flat, not without a key, and even then I'm sure someone would have heard them. It was just a bad dream. Now go to sleep and don't worry. There's a good girl!'

Reluctantly, Jessica let go her grip on Linda's arm, but her small face resumed the tight, pinched look that Linda had almost begun to think of as its normal expression till just recently when with growing confidence in her it had assumed a more childlike expression.

'It's true—it wasn't a dream. There was someone in my room. I know there was,' she

99

reiterated stubbornly before throwing herself down and pulling the bedclothes up tight to her chin. ' 'Night,' she mumbled before closing her eyes in a clear gesture of dismissal.

'Good-night, Jessica. Sleep well!' she said gently before turning and leaving the room with the uncomfortable feeling that she had failed the child.

As usual, it seemed she and Jessica had the flat to themselves, which meant, of course, that she was as firmly trapped as if she were in prison, for there was no way she could leave the child alone.

She went into the lounge and switched through the TV channels. The only programme which held any interest for her at all was the news bulletin and that was nearly over. She watched the last part of it then flicked the screen into blankness once more.

She had only taken in about half of the bit of news she had seen anyway. For some reason she couldn't forget Jessica's insistence that there had really been someone in her room on the previous night and that it was not merely a dream. The thought nagged at her and she realised she should have mentioned this to Bluey. But it seemed such an absurd thing when he was asking her if anything out of the ordinary had happened.

On the other hand, suppose Jessica was telling the truth, and someone had actually been in her room last night. If so, who were they, and what were they up to? By the time her thoughts had reached this point she had worked herself up into such a state of anxiety that she had to get up and tiptoe across the hallway and gently open the child's bedroom door and peer in.

All was well. She could see from the night light that Jessica was asleep. Telling herself she was being over anxious and over imaginative, just like Jessica herself, she made her way back to the lounge.

As she crossed the hallway she passed the phone. Almost without thinking, she stopped and dialled the Bluegums' number. Only as she listened to the ringing tone at the other end of the line and waited for it to be answered did the thought cross her mind that Bluey probably wasn't there. He was almost certainly still in Melbourne. However, to her surprise, he answered the phone.

'Oh, Bluey, it's you. I didn't expect you to be home!' she said, taken by surprise.

'Did you want to talk to Ronnie, Linda?'

'No, it was you I wanted. I just didn't expect you to be there, that's all.'

It didn't occur to her that all that sounded most contradictory.

'What do you want to talk to me about?'

Bluey sounded short. He knew he did and regretted it, but Linda had had every chance to talk to him earlier in the day and had told him nothing. Now here she was on the line just as he got back from a long and tiring drive.

'Well, I should probably have told you,' she began hesitantly before going on to describe Jessica's dream and the child's reaction to it.

'Why couldn't you have told me this today?' Bluey exclaimed and his anger vibrated along the line so that Linda found herself holding the phone a little distance from her ear.

'I'm sorry, but I really didn't think it was important. Then when she started on about it again tonight—'

'Well, thanks for telling me now, anyway!'

Linda did not miss the sarcastic inflection in his voice and found herself looking at the receiver in her hand with a feeling of hurt bewilderment as she heard it crash down at the other end. She was still standing like that when Derek walked in. She turned round, looking the picture of guilt. Her explanation sounded weak, even to her own ears.

'A wrong number—someone had the wrong number,' she murmured as she replaced the receiver.

Even as she spoke, she wondered what had made her lie. Why did her gut feeling assert itself and tell her that Derek should not know that it was Bluey she was talking to on the phone?

'Annoying,' was all he said as he passed her on his way to his office.

He seemed to have accepted her explanation. She heard him moving about and the rustle of papers, then the sound of his briefcase slamming shut before he hurried out and passed her again on his way to the door. If he wondered why she was still standing like some dumbstruck idiot next to the silent phone he made no comment. He seemed too intent on his own business to notice her. All he managed was a perfunctory good-night as the door slammed shut behind him.

She heard the lift door slam and the whine as it descended. Only then did she turn back towards the lounge and at that moment the phone shrilled causing her to actually jump.

'Hello, Bluey! Why are you calling me back?' she asked.

'Linda, please, listen. I was going to say this to you before but you rang off so quickly.'

'Derek was coming in,' she told him and somehow the explanation seemed quite natural and not in the least far-fetched. 'He has gone again now,' she added.

'Good, now listen. Do you think you can sleep in the same room as Jessica tonight?'

'Yes, I guess so,' Linda answered doubtfully.

She would have to wake the child and take her into her own room again she supposed.

'Why? Do you think something is going to happen to her? You don't believe her, do you? You don't think she was right that there was someone in her room?'

'Let's just say I am being cautious. Better to be safe than sorry and all that. By the way, what did Derek come back for?'

'I don't know exactly. He dashed into the office and got some papers and dashed out again. He seemed in a great rush.'

'Would you know what he had taken if you went in and looked?' Bluey asked.

'I doubt it. I have done so little work in there I'm really not too familiar with what's there.'

'Take a look anyway. If you do find out anything call me back. If not, don't bother.'

After she had hung up, Linda did as he asked, but as she had told him she really wasn't too aware of exactly what there was in the office. She looked round and could see nothing gone at first, then she noticed that a folder lay on the top of the filing cabinet as if it had been left out by mistake. She picked it up but it was quite empty so she was no wiser.

There seemed no need to ring Bluey again but she supposed she had better do as he asked about moving Jessica. She went into the child's room and was relieved to see her sleeping peacefully. In fact the very normality of the dimly-lit bedroom and the child in the bed, one arm round her teddy, seemed to make Bluey's request seem absurdly over anxious.

However, Linda walked across to the bed and gently pulled the quilt back. She decided as she looked at Jessica, who appeared dead to the world, that the easiest thing would be to move her without waking her if that were possible. She seemed in a fairly heavy sleep and as she was a small child and Linda reasonably strong she was able to pick her up bodily and carry her next door to her own room and lay her carefully on one side of the double bed without a murmur from her.

Quickly she prepared for bed herself then scrambled in beside the still sleeping child. After propping herself up comfortably with her pillows, she picked up the book that lay on her bedside table. The reading lamp on her side cast most of its light on her half of the bed and did not disturb Jessica who, still clutching her teddy, slept on undisturbed.

Linda read for some time before dozing off over her book. She was startled awake by a bumping sound and what sounded like a muffled curse. At first she thought it was Derek and Marcia returning but the sound did not seem to be coming from the right direction. It was in the room next to hers, Jessica's room!

Without stopping to think, she swung her feet to the floor and padded quietly across the room in her bare feet. Cautiously, she opened the bedroom door a chink. What she saw froze her to the spot. A figure, which she presumed to be male, wearing a stocking mask, was moving swiftly and almost silently, across the lobby to the door, through which, to her immense relief, he disappeared, closing it with a click behind him.

Closing her own door, Linda hurried back to her bed on legs that now seemed to be made of jelly. Having reached its safety she decided that she should do something about her door, but what? It had no lock on it. With a supreme effort of will she climbed out of bed and made her way back across the room. Pulling forward a chair, she wedged it under the doorknob. Jessica's nightmare had now become Linda's reality!

CHAPTER SEVEN

She slept little for the remainder of the night. For the most part she just lay rigid, her ears straining for any untoward sound. Some time in the early hours she heard the front door open and close and the sound of voices.

She guessed that Derek and Marcia were back and the knowledge that she was no longer alone with only a small child and her own fears for company must have relaxed her for she dropped off into an uneasy sleep. She might have remained asleep had it not been for Jessica, awake, bright-eyed and bushy-tailed and astonished to find herself in Linda's bed instead of her own.

'Did I dream again? I don't remember if I did.'

'Uhh, what? No, I just thought maybe you could have been right, so I brought you in here last night,' she explained, trying not to alarm the child.

'I did see a man. I didn't dream it,' Jessica repeated once more, her mouth set in a stubborn line.

'Yes, I'm sure you did.'

Linda did not argue the point with her any more.

'Did you see him, too?'

'Come on, we must hurry and get dressed or

we will be late.'

Linda preferred not to answer the child's question directly, fearing that she might alarm Jessica more. Also at the back of her mind was the odd thought that it might be safer not to talk about the nocturnal visitor. She couldn't give a logical explanation why she thought that. On the face of it, surely it would be wiser to report it to someone. The question was who? Or rather whom could she trust enough to tell?

Bluey came to mind, but he wasn't here to tell. Anyway, she thought, maybe they had, both of them, been imagining things. With the bright morning sun of a new Melbourne day streaming through the window the terror of the previous night did indeed seem more like a nightmare than anything else.

They were just finishing their breakfast and about to set off on the way to the school when Derek came into the kitchen. He was still in pyjamas and dressing-gown and it struck Linda that he looked both tired and harassed.

'Ah, Linda, I'm glad I've caught you before you go. I would like you in the office this morning, so if you could come straight back from school.'

'Yes, of course,' Linda replied.

No chance now of meeting Jane at the coffee bar and maybe getting a message to Bluey or even telephoning him, unless she stopped at a call box on the way home. Her mind ran quickly over the route but she could not recall seeing one. Well, it would have to wait till afternoon or till Derek left the flat, whichever came first. Letting Bluey know about her midnight visitor had suddenly become important.

She hurried Jessica into her school clothes, brushed her hair, made sure she had her lunch box, ran a comb through her own hair, snatched up her hat, glasses and purse, the three things she had come to think of as essentials for walking out in Melbourne, and they set off. As usual, she delivered the child right inside the school premises before leaving. As she walked briskly along, keeping a lookout for a phone booth, she had the uncomfortable feeling that she was not alone.

On the pretext of stopping to look in a shop window, she glanced quickly up the street the way she had come. There were, of course, people there but none who struck her as in any way sinister. However, the unpleasant feeling persisted.

She couldn't resist still glancing back over her shoulder as she hurried along.

There were other people walking the same way as herself, but again, there was nothing that she could see about any one of them that suggested they might be following her.

She didn't see a single public telephone on her walk back. It looked as if she would just have to wait till either she was alone in the flat or could get out on her own to make a call. The uncomfortable feeling of not being alone persisted in spite of the fact that she could see no evidence whatever to the contrary. Nonetheless she was glad when the door of the lift clanged shut and she was on her way up to the flat.

Derek kept her busier than she had been since she first came to Australia, writing letters to his dictation and sorting out some records of some sort of business deal on the computer. Whatever the commodity was she did not know, the wording of the accounts and records seemed so vague.

When she had finished, he asked her to transfer all the work to disks and wipe it from the computer itself.

'Thank you,' he said as he took the disks from her and slipped them into his pocket.

'Are you quite sure you want this all deleted?' she asked him anxiously. 'Suppose you lose the disk?'

'I'm sure!' he all but snapped at her. 'And I have two copies on disk, don't forget. God forbid that I should lose both!'

'That's true,' Linda agreed, then seeing his face darken she added hastily, 'I'm sure you won't.'

She was still closing down the computer when Tina came in with a tray bearing two steaming cups of coffee. As she put them down she said to Derek, 'That is yours, sir.'

Looking up, Linda was in time to see what she could only describe as a meaning look pass between them as Derek took the cup she handed him. The thought crossed her mind that something was going on between these two. Gratefully she took her own coffee, wondering vaguely why Derek had to have a certain one, as they looked identical to her.

'Well,' Derek said and smiled at her with practised charm, 'I think that about wraps up the work in here for today. I've worked you pretty hard, so feel free to relax now till you have to meet Jessica out of school.'

Taking his words as dismissal, Linda got up with a murmured thanks and carried her coffee cup to the lounge where she dropped thankfully into a chair and began to drink it.

It tasted bitter. She must have forgotten to sugar it. She would normally have got up again and gone in search of sugar but she suddenly felt overcome by such a tiredness that she decided to drink it as it was. It must have been the poor night she had endured. Hoping the coffee would revive her she drank deeply.

*　　　*　　　*

'Linda, Miss Linda.'

She opened her eyes in response to the insistent voice somewhere above her. Tina was standing there with her empty cup in her hands.

111

'I'm going now,' she told her and then looked pointedly at her watch. 'I thought I had better wake you up because it is time to get Jessica from school. In fact you are already a few minutes late!'

Linda leaped to her feet, her sleep-blurred thoughts suddenly clearing.

'Oh, good gracious!' she cried, then almost screamed as a small hammer pounded somewhere in her head.

She put her hands up to her temples and shook her head slightly in an attempt to shake herself fully wake. A hollow feeling in her stomach told her she had missed lunch.

'Thanks for waking me, Tina!'

As she hurried out of the flat she thought bitterly, but why couldn't you have done it a bit sooner?

She dashed to the school as fast as she could, almost colliding with other pedestrians and narrowly missed being hit by a car as she tore across a pedestrian crossing on the Don't Walk sign.

At the school, her worst fears were realised. All was deadly quiet. There were no parents' cars waiting and no children in sight. The school doors were still open, however, and she hurried inside and headed for Jessica's classroom. On the way, she collided with her form mistress.

'Jessica?' Linda gasped. 'Where is she?'

'Oh, she's gone already. She went at the

usual time.'

'Gone!'

Linda croaked out the word in horror. Her heart was thudding after her mad dash and her breath came in rasps. Through the panic of the information being imparted to her she was also aware of the steady throbbing of her head. She grabbed the startled teacher's arm in a grip that made the poor woman wince.

'Who picked her up? Who was it?'

'I'm afraid I don't know who she was.'

'She? Can you describe her? Was she smart—sophisticated—around thirty?'

Desperately Linda hoped that it was Marcia and that both she and Jessica were now safely back at the flat having afternoon tea together. Even though the picture of Marcia in this cosy rôle didn't ring at all true she clung to it desperately.

'Oh, no—it was an older woman. I thought it must be her grandmother, as a matter of fact. That's why I didn't worry.'

'I see. Thank you,' Linda replied dully.

It must, Linda thought bitterly, have been someone Jessica knew, but who? The only person who seemed to fit the description was Ronnie, and she was miles away, wasn't she? Part of her wanted to think it was Ronnie, but if it was, then it meant that she couldn't be trusted, and if she couldn't then could Bluey?

She threw one last despairing look round the school as if by some magic Jessica might suddenly materialise, before wearily setting off back to the flat. How was she going to admit to Derek that she had let his daughter be kidnapped because she had been asleep and therefore late to pick her up?

As she walked slowly back churning over and over in her mind just what she was going to say, a last glimmer of hope shot through her agonised thoughts. Maybe, just maybe, it was someone sent by Derek himself to pick Jessica up and she would find her there safe and sound when she got back. But her hopes were soon dashed. When she let herself in she could hear voices in the lounge.

Marcia and Derek were there calmly drinking tea. They both looked up expectantly when she walked into the room.

'Where's Jessica?'

It was Marcia, who usually never seemed to care whether the child was there or not, who asked the question. Linda looked from one to the other in despair.

'Isn't she here?' she asked dully.

Derek shot to his feet so suddenly that he almost knocked over the small table by his side.

'Are you saying you don't know where she is—that you have lost her?' he demanded in a voice that seemed to cut like cold steel.

Linda nodded miserably.

'Yes,' she mumbled.

She could think of nothing else to say.

There was no possible excuse she could make for the truth, that she had been asleep when it was time to fetch her from school.

'How very careless!' Marcia drawled.

Surprised by the comment, Linda looked directly at her and was shocked by the gleam of amusement that shot through the malice in the unwavering stare with which she met Linda's eyes. Feeling as if she had been physically slapped, Linda turned away. She had little choice anyway for Derek was once more addressing her in that cold, surprisingly calm, voice.

'Were you late getting to the school?'

Linda nodded miserably.

'I see. And she had already gone when you got there?'

Again Linda nodded.

'Of course, there is always the possibility that she is on her way home somewhere by herself.'

Derek seemed to be talking to himself as much as anyone else. Linda shook her head.

'No, she was picked up. The teacher told me so.'

With every word she was forced to speak Linda felt the weight of her guilt grow heavier. For the umpteenth time she wondered how on earth she had managed to drop off to sleep so heavily that she missed lunch and had to be woken several hours later by Tina. The only explanation was the fact that she had so little sleep last night.

'Hadn't we better inform someone?' she suggested hesitantly.

'Yes, yes, of course. Marcia, would you—'

He shot the other woman an intense look across the room which Linda took to be an expression of his concern.

'Of course,' Marcia drawled before getting up in her usually languid way and strolling out of the room, closing the door behind her.

Linda heard the sound of the phone being lifted before Derek claimed her attention once more.

'I'm sure you realise, Linda, that after this I cannot continue to employ you,' he said calmly, and coldly.

Linda looked up sharply. In her initial distress and concern for Jessica this aspect of things simply had not crossed her mind.

'Of course, I will pay your salary up to the end of the month and pay your return air fair back to England,' he went on.

Linda continued to stare at him. He couldn't mean this surely! He was just going to send her back to England, just like that?

'But—' she said feebly.

'I'll arrange for a flight for you as soon as possible. I suggest you get packed ready as I may be able to get you on a plane tomorrow.'

Linda just gaped at him. She couldn't believe this was happening. A child was missing—lost—possibly kidnapped—in this big city and all her father could think about was getting rid of the so-called carer who had allowed this to happen. In fact that seemed his first priority, not the recovery of his child.

Striving to maintain her dignity she mumbled, 'Thank you,' and stumbled away to her own room. Even allowing for the fact that grief and shock could affect people in very different ways, Linda found it hard to understand his attitude. All she could think was that he was so upset that he simply could no longer bear to see the person responsible for what had happened.

With a feeling of utter despair she threw her clothes into her case without much care, her only concern to ram them in and get the lid down. So much for her idea of adventure in Australia. If this was it, then she wanted no part of it and wished she had stayed back home.

In spite of her own worries and the concern she felt about Jessica, Linda dropped into a fitful sleep that night full of disturbing dreams. When she was wakened by a hand over her mouth, she did not realise at first that she was awake or she might have died of terror.

A torch was shining on her so that she couldn't see her assailant properly, but as far as she could make out it was the same masked figure she had caught a glimpse of the night before and that Jessica had described seeing the night before that.

Pointing with the hand holding the torch, he indicated she was to get out of bed. Almost too scared to move but more afraid to disobey, Linda sat up. She opened her mouth to scream but seemed to have lost her voice and before she could find even a croak, the figure standing over her had dropped the torch on the bed and wound some sort of scarf round her mouth and was dragging her to the door.

He picked up her clothes lying over a chair on the way and thrust them into her arms, grabbed her handbag, put the shoulder strap over her head and, holding her free hand with one of his, he snatched up her suitcase with the other. He opened the door cautiously, looked out then made a dash across the hallway. Still feeling that she was in a nightmare, Linda found herself outside the building and pushed into a car waiting at the kerb with the engine running.

The driver did not turn but began to rev up the car. Her captor slammed the door shut, with her suitcase still in his hand, saluted the driver and they were off. Linda put her hand up and easily pulled off the scarf round her mouth. Then, quite calmly, as if she were out on a Sunday afternoon drive, she reached for her seat-belt and clicked it round her.

All the time, she felt as if she were not there but watching herself in some curious dream state. It was not unlike the way she had felt on her arrival in Australia when she was suffering from jet lag. She settled back in her seat and made herself comfortable. She studied the back view of the driver, a slight person with a baseball cap pulled down over their head and wearing a dark parka. As, even at this time of night, it was not cold Linda presumed it was some sort of cover-up.

In a detached way, she wondered why she wasn't frightened, at least not as frightened as she had been last night in the flat when she had spied on the intruder through the chink in the door. Now that all her worst fears had become reality it seemed rather pointless to be afraid.

She must have dozed off because when she next looked around her, the city had given way to the northbound highway and open country. She was startled into full awareness when a pleasant female voice asked, 'Are you awake, Linda?'

'Jane!' She gasped. 'What—where—?'

There were so many questions milling in her mind she didn't know which to ask first.

'We're going to Bluegums,' Jane replied calmly as if they were making the most normal journey in the world.

'Would you like to sit in the front? If you are fully awake and would like to talk it would be more comfortable.'

She pulled the car into a parking bay and opened the front passenger door for Linda to move.

'I have a flask of coffee here if you would like a cup,' she said.

They sat in a companionable silence for a few minutes drinking the hot coffee. Linda was trying to sort out the many questions and decide which she wanted to ask first.

'Jessica?' she asked finally. 'Do you know anything about her?'

'Quite a bit. Don't worry—she is quite safe. As a matter of fact she is at Bluegums with Ronnie.'

Of course, Linda thought, remembering the teacher's description of the woman who had picked the child up from school.

'But what do you have to do with all this?' she asked Jane.

'I'm Jessica's mother,' was the astonishing answer.

'Her mother! But—'

'I met you because I wanted to check you out—see what sort of a person was in charge of my child,' Jane told her. 'It was essential that I wasn't seen by Jessica. She was convinced I was safely out of the way in England.'

Linda felt more confused than ever as Jane matter of factly told her this. Where, she wondered, did Bluey fit into all this. And why had she been kidnapped and why were they all heading for Bluegums?

'Was it Ronnie who collected Jessica from school?' she asked now.

'Of course. I thought you realised that. She has known Jessica since she was a baby. She loves her like her own and that is why she agreed to stay on at Bluegums as housekeeper for Derek.'

Linda was still floundering.

'Jane, do you think you could explain things to me from the beginning, slowly and carefully so that I can understand?'

Jane laughed.

'OK, I'll tell you about my part in it anyway, starting from the beginning. Derek is my husband—ex-husband, I should say. Bluegums is actually my property. It is the home where I was brought up. Derek was first employed by my father as manager, then Dad died quite suddenly. Mum was already dead, while I was at college in England.

'It seemed simplest to let Derek go on managing things, simple, too, and at the time the right thing, to marry him. He can be very charming, you know. Well, Jessica was born a year after we were married. Ronnie was there even before that. She was Dad's housekeeper and she stayed on and kept things going for Derek. I asked her to stay after we were married, so, as I said, she has known Jessica all her life.

'I knew Jessica loved and trusted her and would willingly go with her. Well, by the time Jessica was a year old, our marriage was well and truly falling to bits, partly because Derek was seldom there and also I was getting worried because there always seemed so much money.'

'That seems a funny thing to worry about. For most people it is the other way around!' Linda remarked dryly.

'I know, but I knew just how Dad had been doing on the property and how much money he was making and it was nothing like the amount Derek always seemed to have. I wondered about the time he spent in Melbourne, too, and the overseas trips he took—trips he certainly didn't want me on. Quite by chance I stumbled on the secret of his wealth—drugs.

'He was running a huge racket. Unfortunately I was fool enough to let him know I knew and the upshot of it was he used Jessica as a means of blackmailing me. I kept quiet and out of his way, that meant away from Bluegums, of course, or something would happen to Jessica.'

'But she is his daughter!' Linda said aghast.

'Exactly, and of course he may well have been bluffing, but I couldn't take the chance so I did what he asked, on the surface anyway. Fortunately, Dad had left me some money as well as the property so I took myself to the appropriate authorities and told them what I suspected and they had him watched. Just to make sure, I got an undercover man as well. He got a job at Bluegums as manager as he had impeccable qualifications from an English Agricultural College before he thought farming was too tame and did a spell in the police.'

'Bluey?' Linda asked softly.

'Of course—the same!'

'Where is he now? Is he at Bluegums, too?'

'Not quite,' Jane answered dryly. 'After kidnapping you he went back to tie things up, or to be more accurate, to get Derek tied up.'

'You mean, it was Bluey at the flat?' Linda cried. 'I didn't know, but he was masked and never spoke!'

Perhaps this explained why she had not been totally terror stricken!

They lapsed into a sympathetic silence. There were many more questions Linda wanted to ask but she decided that most of them could wait for Bluey. But there was more she had to know about Jessica's kidnapping.

'It seemed to me that Derek wasn't as worried as he should have been about Jessica, and—well—I know it sounds far-fetched but I think I was doped to make me sleep.'

'Of course you were! And as for Derek, well, the joke is he had arranged for Jessica to be snatched and when it happened he didn't realise that it wasn't his man who had her!'

Linda laughed, as much in relief that she hadn't been neglectful of her small charge as much as anything.

'If he had asked me for a description of the person who picked her up I suppose he would have guessed,' she mused.

'He would,' Jane agreed. 'Fortunately he was so confident that it was his plan in action!'

As she spoke, dawn was breaking and the stand of magnificent blue gum trees that gave the property its name were silhouetted against the sky, appearing to Linda like some message of hope.

*   *   *

She slept late next morning and when she put in an appearance it was to find Jane and Ronnie drinking coffee in the kitchen in a sort of tense silence. Jessica was happily colouring in on the other side of the table.

'Hi, Linda,' she said cheerfully.

Linda looked from one to the other of the two women.

'We're waiting for news,' Jane explained.

At that exact moment the phone rang and Jane raced to answer it. Her face was one beam of relief when she came back.

'That was Bluey,' she told them, rather unnecessarily. 'He is on his way here. We can all relax. Derek and the rest of his lot have all been arrested. Bluey wants to talk to you, Linda.'

She rushed to the phone almost as fast as Jane had done before her.

'Bluey!'

Her voice sounded breathless and her heart

was hammering in the oddest way.

'Linda, I'm on my way. I just wanted to check that you had survived your kidnapping.'

'I've survived! When will you be here?'

'In about half an hour. I'm talking on the mobile phone.'

It seemed a long half hour to Linda and when he finally arrived, she had to wait until after lunch before she could fire the many questions at him that still burned in her mind.

'I'm going to see the horses,' he said to her as he got up from the table. 'Come and talk to Molly, Linda.'

They leaned on the yard gate with the soft warm breath of the horses scenting the air as they nuzzled hopefully for titbits.

'Can you explain just why you had to kidnap me, Bluey?'

'For your safety. You were part of the scheme. Your failing to collect Jessica and subsequent dismissal was a put-up job. You were doped so that you would sleep and miss her coming out of school. Jessica was supposed to be kidnapped, but not by Ronnie.'

Linda nodded.

'So Jane said.'

'Fortunately, Derek didn't realise at the time that it was our person, not his who had the child, which is why he was relatively calm about the whole thing. The plan was that she would be snatched for twenty-four hours by one of his people and then returned safe and sound, but in the meantime you would have been sacked and despatched with great haste on the next plane back to England.'

'But why?' Linda stammered.

'In your suitcase, my dear Linda, was hidden a sizeable packet of drugs. You were the innocent carrier. It was unlikely you would be searched but if you were, then you would carry the can. That was the plan.'

'Oh, gosh!'

Linda felt the childish exclamation hardly did justice to what she felt as she realised the enormity of what she had escaped.

'Fortunately we got wind of it all and foiled it quite nicely. Our friend, Derek, is where he can't do any harm to anyone tonight!'

'Is that why my case didn't make it into the car with me?'

'Absolutely! But it is here now and only contains what it should. The packet was hidden in the lining where it had been carefully sewn in by Tina while you were out of the flat.'

'Oh!' was all Linda seemed able to exclaim weakly.

Then as another thought occurred to her she looked up into the vivid blue eyes and something in them made her heart jump.

'What happens now?'

He put his hands on her shoulders.

'That depends on you, Linda. You can return to England, or you can stay on here.'

'But what about you?' she whispered.

'I've decided I've had enough of drama and excitement. Jane has asked me if I will stay here as manager, for real.'

'And are you?'

'I haven't decided. It depends on you. Do you think you could bear to make your home here, to help me run this place?'

At this moment Molly gave her a nudge with her soft muzzle.

'She would like you to as well!' Bluey laughed.

'I think I could bear it,' she told him.

'On a permanent basis?'

'I reckon!' she told him.

Fleetingly, as his lips met hers, she remembered that she had finished with men—for ever.

'Oh, Bluey!' she murmured as her arms slid up round his neck, and as he pulled her close, she knew that here was one she could trust—always and for ever.

We hope you have enjoyed this Large
Print book. Other Thorndike Press or
Chivers Press Large Print books are
available at your library or directly from
the publishers.

For more information about current and
upcoming titles, please call or write,
without obligation, to:

Thorndike Press
295 Kennedy Memorial Drive
Waterville, Maine 04901
Tel. (800) 223-1244
OR
Chivers Large Print
published by BBC Audiobooks Ltd
St James House, The Square
Lower Bristol Road
Bath BA2 3BH
England
Tel. (0)225 335336

All our Large Print titles are designed for
easy reading, and all our books are made
to last.